THE INCONVENIENCE OF THE WINGS

SILAS DENT ZOBAL

Fomite
Burlington, VT

Stories from this collection have appeared in the following publications. The author expresses his gratitude to the supportive editors of: *Glimmer Train, New Orleans Review; Shenandoah; Beloit Fiction Journal; Iron Horse Review; Wisconsin Review; North American Review; Green Mountains Review; Peculiar Pilgrims*, and the *Missouri Review.*

ISBN-13: 978-1-942515-01-2
Library of Congress Control Number: 2015933332

Fomite
58 Peru Street
Burlington, VT 05401
www.fomitepress.com

For my mom, Susan Therese Gehring

Contents

Camp of Low Angels

We send the children out on missions. Out you go, we say, out to build teepees from pine poles and wool blankets. Out to howl like a wolf, whine like a coyote, growl like a bear. Out to glean an understanding of tragedy through skinned knees. Pick blackberries for blackberry pie. Plant roadside tomato, cucumber, green pepper seeds. Demonstrate how to remove leeches with a waterproof match. Point out the high grasses infested with ticks. Observe how a magnifying glass can turn sunshine into fire. Notice the reddish color of the ground. Realize the earth is heavy with clay. Eat wild blueberries until fingers turn maroon. Decorate the lodges in nature scenes cut from construction paper. Lie on picnic tables and watch for satellites, shooting stars, comets. Dance round the bonfire. Make ice cream.

We stay inside to contemplate guide books. We are counselors, we wear brown uniforms, we feel we have a certain standard of dignity to uphold. We write our morning speeches in longhand and find ourselves inspired. Find a centipede, we say, a gypsy moth, a carpenter ant, a wolf spider, a garter snake. Yes, we tell Johnny Millwood, alive. *Please, Johnny, alive.*

Find rocks that look to have come from the moon. See how twenty arms can lift Ozzy Green high above little heads. Draw a family tree and then climb it. Don't speak for an entire day. Examine the geodesic dome we call the Mess Hall. Identify dogwood, cottonwood, cypress, oak, cedar, willow. Paddle a canoe across the Kishwaukee river at sunset. Wear a life jacket. Invent a language with your trusted friends. Distinguish between deciduous and evergreen. Remember how white berries are never to be eaten. Write down dirty jokes and burn the lined paper in the campfire. Wear white on Monday and black on Friday to celebrate and mourn the passage of time. Draw maps of all the routes between the lodges and the latrine. Build a fort in an apple tree. Use a compass to find north. Reflect on the forces that can rend a heart in two. Watch a caterpillar form a cocoon. Fish for bluegill before sunrise. Find fossils and identify them. Hunt for arrowheads and round civil war bullets near the site where a fort once stood. Come upon a geode and discuss how certain people exist who, like the geode, don't reveal their glory until they're broken. Learn to weave complicated structures out of yarn. Use fingers as joinery. Take apart owl pellets and reconstruct mouse bones, find translucent snake skins, stumble upon elk antlers. Know that these are the times that will later haunt you. Sleep in the wide open. Understand that dirt smells different when wet. Taste wild mint, clover, rose hips. Chew grass as an announcement that you have nothing better to do. Commune with nature until the tap-tap of the woodpecker rhymes with your pulse. Learn how to make chicken noodle soup, how to cook flat bread, how pepperoni and cheese suits anybody after a day's hike. Learn to tell time by the lines in your palm, how to walk without sound. Make wings out of branches and oak leaves. Memorize a new song. Chart the stars.

This is Camp Winnebago and this is your mission.

When, over oatmeal and peaches at breakfast, we relay how they shouldn't ever, *never ever,* pick their noses in public, Adam O'Rourke asks, how about his bottom? The children find this uproarious. We say it's best to avoid even speaking of the nether regions, young Mr. O'Rourke.

Johnny Millwood tells us how we're better than his father any day. We clap one another's shoulders and say we have set the standard for well done. Good god! we deserve a thousand rewards. As counselors we bring a stylish bearing to our brown uniforms. This is a course that history has never taken before. Patrick Levin desists in his bed wetting. Eddie Mundoon stops screaming in the night. We stand straight, we swagger. Write, we instruct, true stories from your neighborhoods to be shared around the campfire.

The word of the day is contentment. Theodore Muntz relents and makes his bed. Little Adam O'Rourke, too short for his age, grows a good two centimeters taller. In the latrine, we admit to ourselves that the children have grown close to our hearts. We've done the impossible, we have. Ozzy Green, who previously would scream at the sight of a hairbrush, compromises and agrees to comb his cowlicked hair. As a present, Aaron Bushel carves us fish hooks out of wood. Manny Pulinski draws and colors a highly detailed map of the world to be hung in the Mess Hall. A group of children led by Philip Bell sculpt a totem pole with hatchets. Theodore Muntz vows to masturbate less frequently. Good Theodore, we say, *bravo!* Camp Winnebago gives him a round of applause.

THEN THEODORE MUNTZ SAYS WE STINK. That's right stink, he says, stank, stunk. We scowl. Stink how? we ask ourselves. We shower before supper and after supper. We rub our skin raw. We iron our uniforms mercilessly. Theodore Muntz says our stink, stank, stunk runs deeper.

We say, right after the campfire, Theodore Muntz, you'll go to bed early. We notice T.J. Wilde insists on carrying a yardrule over his shoulder. Someone starts a rumor saying it's used to scare the littlest children. Theodore Muntz shows off a dead robin. Johnny Millwood hits Theodore with his moonrock. We argue whether young Millwood's behavior is a problem or just qualifies as precocious.

Gathered around the fire in pajamas, the children read their neigh-

borhood stories aloud. Adam O'Rourke tells how his next door neighbor
never goes outside, only sits in a lightless room in front of a pocket-sized
television, eating spaghetti and meatballs out of a can.

Manny Pulinski says he's nothing to tell about his neighbors, they're all
ignoramuses. The children's eyes hold a frightening animal gleam.

Theodore Muntz says one day he looked out the window and every last
neighbor had packed up and departed to destinations unknown.

Johnny Millwood relates how the neighbor's iguana, Maurice, crawled
into the infrastructure of his mother's Volkswagen, died, decayed, and
began to stink so rotten they had to drive with the sunroof open, windows down, handkerchiefs wrapped around their faces like bandits. Even
in winter.

Theodore Muntz bets Johnny Millwood a slice of blueberry pie that our
stink's worse than Maurice's. Any day. Johnny Millwood says his mother
hung a dozen deodorant Jesuses, poured bleach into available crevasses,
and eventually gave the Volkswagen away to a man who had lost half his
face in the second World War.

A baker's dozen children sit listlessly on felled logs. The lodges reek of
dried urine. At night twenty anonymous arms take to lifting Ozzy Green
and dropping him on rocks. Ozzy, we say, you can talk to us. Word among
the children is that Ozzy has decided never to speak again. Theodore
Muntz gathers thirty children, divides them into nose- vs. butt-pickers,
talks them up, and starts a rock fight between them. We begin to suspect
the children swear at us in a few dozen invented languages. Aaron Bushel
shaves Ozzy Green bald. T.J. Wilde sets fire to the apple tree.

We agree that the nightly dance around the bonfire has taken on a grisly
spirit. It gives us goose bumps. Eddie Mundoon tells how, kittycorner from
his house, two children live in the root cellar. They go naked and sometimes roll in their barren lawn for fun. Their parents are hollow-eyed, pale
as winter, and allow the children inside their home only when relatives
arrive. Eddie would watch them being shoved into dresses and slacks like

marionettes, hair cut and combed, settled into kitchen chairs, and screamed at to clean their plates of peas during supper.

Rich Kent says his sister decided she liked to kiss girls, not boys, and his parents told her to live on the street. The street wasn't much good to her, Rich Kent says, she'd been so upset she'd stopped eating altogether and started injecting poisonous liquids straight into her veins.

Good lord! we say.

Donnie Farkle says his neighbors howl at night. Like whupped dogs. Which sometimes makes him wet the bed.

Buzz DeLint relates how his parents purchased an olive-skinned foreigner to take care of the housework and make her sleep in the shed.

Oh, we say, how ghastly! We suggest a sing-a-long. Maybe Johnny Appleseed?

We counselors, we confer and decide there isn't crap to be done about it. That's what we decide. Simply can't be helped. We put all our eggs in one basket and the bottom gave out. Right? we say, *right?* Every last one of them, we say to ourselves, needs a hiding. We debate who has the sturdiest leather belt for strapping. We decide any resort to the physical would be just plain wrong. The set-an-example cliché gets bandied about like a Frisbee. We discuss tying a number of children to their beds. We remind ourselves how we know knots.

The stories cannot be stopped from coming. We set a seven o'clock curfew. We patrol. We start rumors of a dungeon. We put the chief mischief-makers in one lodge and watch the doors. Chocolates are offered as incentives for those who don't throw rocks. Johnny Millwood begins a mud war. We practice scowls before the latrine mirror. We call a camp meeting in the Mess Hall to lecture on the nature of authority, the futility of resistance, the inevitability of surrender. Theodore Muntz pounds on the table and begins a chant of *Screw you!* Someone throws a soup spoon. The key lime pie scheduled for dessert is not served. Off to bed, we say, guardians will most certainly be informed. Fear delayed reprisals, we say. The children bundle off to bed, many of them howling. Animals, we whisper among ourselves, beasts and mental cripples. Symptoms indicate a deficiency in parenting we announce. Yes, *yes*, we clap one another on the back. Buck up, we say.

Above his lodge's entrance way, Buzz DeLint pastes a penis cut from red construction paper. Theodore Muntz clogs all the toilets in the latrine with Camp Winnebago t-shirts, and most of the boys begin crapping in our finest canoe. We find Adam O'Rourke puking in our shoes. We notice how our heads itch with lice. T.J. Wilde starts a bonfire in the poop canoe and sets it adrift on the Kishwaukee River.

We console one another by saying we hadn't bargained on an arsonist in our midst.

Rich Kent says his neighbor has lived one-hundred-and-two years and does nothing with his remaining hours but sob.

Philip Bell says he lives in the country. He doesn't have any neighbors. He doesn't have any brothers or sisters. His mama died in a train accident, his papa lost a leg.

It's okay, Philip, we say, it *is* okay.

Philip says it's not okay with him.

Johnny Millwood tells how a mother and two little girls who lived next to him were butchered by their father with an army-issue shovel. He can still see the blood splattered on the inside of the windows. He's tracing patterns in the air with an index finger.

Stop, we say, *stop*!

We suggest an expedition to gather four-leaf clovers, but Donnie Farkle spits on our shoes. T.J. Wilde calls Patrick Levin a butt licker. We pry the lighter from T.J. Wilde's grubby paws. We find ourselves forced to restrain Patrick Levin by twisting his arm. We sit on Theodore Muntz until he cries uncle.

T.J. Wilde force-feeds bald Ozzy Green a handful of white berries. The berries cause Ozzy to hallucinate. Adam O'Rourke pisses in our pot of chicken noodle soup. Ozzy Green scales the mess hall and jumps from its peak with oak-leaf wings. Ozzy dislocates his shoulder. Outside the Counselor's Lodge, Johnny Millwood sets booby traps that hoist us, feet first, into trees. You little *shit!* we say, you're dead. A hundred eyes turn our way. Hands cover mouths.

We're gonna tell, the children say.

In the latrine, we bite our knuckles. We wipe our faces with wrinkled brown camp uniforms. We tell ourselves we look stalwart. We stand before the children and say we are sorry, *so sorry*. We take to our knees. We're inappropriate. We're sad.

It's okay, they say, much better than last year.

We lower the Camp Winnebago flag to half mast. Someone has used it to wipe their bottom.

You just don't get us, they say. We insist it's they who do not understand us. We are certain of it. Hey, they say, no hard feelings. We shake hands and have fudgesicles all around. T.J. Wilde says all of us are in the same poop canoe. We hug.

Tell us, Adam O'Rourke says. What? we ask. Stories, he says.

All of us sit on the ground. In a circle. We tell how we're seen a neighbor child burying a headless cat. There's a man we know who has artificial legs. How we found a human skeleton buried in our lawn. How once we saw a father drag his boy and a beagle into the backyard and snap the dog's spine over his knee. We fall silent.

You forgive us? we say.

Forgive *what?* say the children. Philip Bell pats our shoulders and says everything will turn out okay. Theodore Muntz says he's thinking of a few things we could do. By way of making it up.

The children send us out on missions. Get Jujubes, they say, S'mores, Icy Pops. Never heard of them, we say. Get them anyway. There is this matter of sending a letter to each parent telling how we believe their child to really actually be an angel. Pick up giant cans of Fruit Cocktail, Frosted Flakes, jawbreakers the size of our heads. Get a supply of saltwater taffy, of rubber footballs, of resiliency. Get ready to dance with them around the campfire. Get ready to whoop and holler.

Hear that? we say, maybe we taught them the word *resiliency*.

Go ahead, they say, get something for yourselves.

We make haste. We slap our thighs. We go. We get.

The Bellwether

Any one might be one coming to be almost an old one. Any one might be one coming to be an old one. Any one might be one coming to be a dead one.
— Gertrude Stein

WHEN SARAH MIDDLEMASS DIED we wrapped her in a red bed sheet. We carried her by her head and her feet and put her on the couch. The radio, turned on in the farmhouse kitchen, forecast days of heavy snowfall; the driveway was an impasse; the nearest farm lay five miles away. We stood there. The couch was old leather. The body lay beneath the red sheet. We—Donny, Patti and me—bundled up and went outside. The snow fell in clumps. The drifts came to our chests and were still rising. Ice splintered across the farmhouse windows. Wind whistled under the eaves. Slat-limbed trees quivered. We waded back and forth between the barn and the house to keep warm. With each step we sunk to mid-thigh in snow. We argued quietly about what to do with the body. We chaffed each other's hands and shoulders. We stayed outside. We hung an electric lantern from the hook on the barn door, and we left it on.

"WHAT IN HELL do we do with her?" I said.

"What do you mean?" Patti asked. "There's nothing to do."

"We can't leave her in the house," said Donny.

"He's right," I said.

"Why not?" asked Patti.

"I'm afraid to sleep," Donny said.

As A WINTER VACATION, the four of us—Donny and Sarah, Patti and me—had planned a week on my aunt's farm: an eighteenth-century stone house with dense hills, sledding and snowshoeing, tea by the hearth. We drove to the farm in light snow. We bundled in clothes like children. We exclaimed at the crystallization of our breath in the air. We ran about in the snow. That first night, we bundled up when the blizzard set in. We cramped under blankets before the fire. Patti held my thigh. Donny cupped Sarah's cold hands.

"I DIDN'T REALLY EVEN LIKE HER," said Patti.

"I thought you did," Donny said.

"Not really. You did?"

"I guess I did."

"I didn't really know her," I said.

"Did you want to?" Donny asked.

"No. I guess. Not really."

WE SHOVELED. Wind harried the snow in horizontal gusts. We channeled between the house and the barn: the snow even with my navel, the sky a vertiginous swirl, the air scented of cold. Through the front window, under a cone of yellow light, was Sarah's body wrapped in the red sheet. Patti slammed her shovel into the snow and leaned against the wind. She wore a stitched leather hat, a wool scarf, a gray jacket with fur bristling around the hood. Hers was a military beauty: hard and even bones; a loud, sharp voice. She was relentless in her shoveling.

I took frequent rests. Donny brought us cups of hot cocoa. His back was like a range of weathered mountains. He wore a ski coat. Circles could describe him: round back and belly, round head, round ears and mouth. Our boots were ringed with packed snow. We avoided the house; we shoveled faster to stay warm.

"I've known her less than a month," Donny said.

"What're you telling me that for?" I asked. "You introduced her to Patti and me last week. This shit is your fault."

"Don't put this on me."

"Jesus, what was wrong with her?"

"I don't know," Danny said. "Nothing, I don't think."

"*Something* was wrong with her."

"Seizures. I think she said she used to have seizures."

We finished the channel between the barn and the house. There was ice at our feet, packed snow at our sides, clouds above. In the house: the fire crackled in the hearth; the radio played cello; the indoor heat hurt our faces. We gathered Sarah's body in the red bed sheet. We hefted. We slipped along our tunnel. We did not speak. The electric lantern shone on the barn door. In the crossing, a half-inch of snow accumulated on top of Sarah. We brushed the sheet off with bare hands. We brushed the snow from each other. We wandered about the barn, then cleared a corner of cobwebs. We laid her in an old, tin trough. We unwrapped the red sheet. Half-light filtering through the barn door; dust-gray bottles lined the windows; the muted sound of heavy snowfall; the stacks of hay; the dirt floor. Beneath the sheet, the shining blue-white of skin. I can't remember her face. Sarah lay dead in the barn for five days.

"I can't remove the image from my head," Patti said.

"Sarah?" I asked.

"Of course, Sarah."

"What image is it?"

"In the barn. In the trough. Frozen."

In bed, Patti's skin felt synthetic. Her arms were rubbery. Outside the window, snow still fell and the light on the barn door lightly glowed. Our hands were against one another's skin. Sometimes, one or the other of us was crying. I asked her if she thought our entire bodies could be prosthetics. She opened her knees. In the dark, her skin outshone the nightlight; her unblinking, lambent eyes; the white of her teeth. The sheets beneath us felt slippery. She pulled me to her; she asked if we even really liked each other. I put my mouth against her. She didn't think so, she said, we never liked each other. Her hands gripped my upper arms so they hurt. She said we weren't any good together. With my head to her breast, I heard her blood moving. She put the small of my ear in her mouth. Her mouth was bigger than I remembered. We smelled like blood, or warmth, or dirt. She moved beneath me; her skin slid against mine. We made sounds.

"It's a perfectly decent sheet," Patti said.

"No, it isn't," said Donny. "It's red."

"Look at it, goddamnit," I said. "It's like she's bloody."

Donny drove us to the cemetery—the three of us. It was late afternoon. We took a highway. The buildings alongside the highway were grayish or off-white. The snow was white. The cars around us were all gray or black or white. The road pooled with melting snow. Donny drove; Patti took the front passenger seat; I sat in the back behind Donny's seat. Donny's hair looked like a mass of weeds and burrs. That highway was a road I'm not familiar with. I asked Donny, and then Patti, if they recognized any of this road. Both of them shook their heads no. I kept touching Patti's shoulder over the back of her seat, and she kept brushing my hand away.

No one could talk over the hum of wheels against cement. The empty seat beside me bore the impression of a person, a gentle declivity marking an absent back, hips, legs. Outside, a trio of pigeons glided over telephone wires. The road was gray, and the sky was an inchoate mess of gray clouds. Donny's sedan was red. I pictured someone's high-above view of our red car. I hit my closed fist against the door's inner panel.

On the far side of the highway, in the oncoming traffic, a slowing white pickup—its taillights luminescent—passed us by. The driver was a lone woman wearing a red scarf. I watched from the rear window. The pick-up stopped for an ambulance passing on the left. There was no siren. The only sound was the hum of the road.

"This car is goddamn ridiculous."

"This car?" Donny said. "I love this car."

"It's absurd. Isn't it, Patti? Tell him. It's absurd."

"What's so ridiculous?" Donny said.

"Functionally," said Patti, "it's an adequate car."

"Functionally," I said, "it's pissing me off. It's goddamn red."

"Red?" Donny said. "So what? It's a good color."

"What I suggest—" Patti said.

"This criticism of my car is making me sad," Donny said. He hit the steering wheel with a palm.

"Nobody ever seems to listen," Patti said.

"Oh, for Christ's sake!" I said. "Pull the fuck over."

For five days at the farmhouse, I shoveled the ice channel. We sat around the woodstove near the kitchen. We built fires, made tea, drank gin and tonics. We played card games. Spades. Gin rummy. Hearts. We talked whether we ought to cook baked potatoes or scalloped. We talked about our favorite lettuces: romaine, Bibb, radicchio, arugula. We talked about the electric lantern hanging from the barn door. We talked about how

Donny had stopped showering. We talked about how long it might snow. We talked loudly without listening to one another about what a mess we were in. We argued about whether or not we could just leave her out there, without checking, without making sure. We argued about what there was to be sure of. Patti yelled; I cursed; Donny cried. We settled down; we touched one another's shoulders or hands. We talked about the last time we remembered Sarah turning toward each of us. The flip of her dark hair. The way she had of tilting her head slightly to one side as she looked at you. The single raised eyebrow. The half-smile.

"The fucking phone's still not fucking working," I said.

"Calm down," Patti said. "She's dead. A delay in a telephone call isn't hurting anyone."

"I don't fucking like her out there."

"Can you think of a better place?"

"Farther away from me."

Getting out of Donny's sedan, I walked to the cemetery. Donny and Patti drove off. My shoes had pointed toes and leather bottoms. My scarf felt like a noose—the ends trailed in the wind. Poplars lined the road. Salt crystals puddled the shoveled sidewalk. A line of stone and brick houses faced the cemetery. Those old masonries were composed of bits of rectangular stone or fired clay and mortar. The chimneys of the houses I walked past were crumbling. I wondered where the word *mortar* came from. What might mortar be made from? How long could such old mortar hold? Ahead, a bony ancient oak tree grew by the wrought-iron entrance gate. Clouds masked the sky. The cold seeped under the hem of my overcoat and tunneled through the cuffs. Donny's red car turned into the entrance. I stopped. How many steps lay between the cemetery gate and me?

Maybe I shouldn't have gone into that cemetery. Maybe I should have turned around, walked away. I had barely known Sarah. Or maybe I ought to have hopped the chainlink fence to my left, pushed through the snow, and arrived at the grave covered in dirt and slush.

To my left sat windowless mausoleums, stone crosses, pointed obelisks, marbled statuary. The red sedan disappeared into the cemetery's fir trees. The sky swirled with filigreed ice. The branches rustled in the trees, and night threatened to fold over us like dark wings.

"Remember how you said you hadn't wanted to know her?" Donny asked.

"That's not quite what I said, I don't think," I said.

"Anyway, how do you feel now?"

"Now?"

"With her in the ground."

"Right now I wish I'd known her," I said.

"Me too," said Patti.

Sarah had purchased the groceries: butterfly pork chops, chicken breasts, rye bread, butter, cheese, sausage, milk, red peppers, zucchini, Portobello mushrooms, marrowfat peas. In the farmhouse, drinking rum and coke, we had long talks about ritual, and, while Patti and Donny fixed dinner, I would go out to re-shovel the channel. The snow was wet and heavy. I'd sweat despite the cold. When I was through, I'd salt the ground. Through the kitchen window, I could watch Donny fixing the main courses and Patti fixing the vegetables.

On my return from the channel, I set three plates, three napkins, three sets of silverware. I washed my hands and face. I sat at the table. The shoveling took me away from the transfiguration of Sarah's groceries: the boiling of peas; the melting of butter in a saucepan; and, on the cutting block, the wet meat.

"I'm not sure this is working." I said.

"What?" Patti asked.

"This whatever-you-call-it. This thing. Us."

"I wasn't sure there was a thing," she said.

"Sure there was."

"This thing—it's dead too?"

"Maybe. I don't know."

"I'll tell you what," Patti said, "you're getting on my nerves."

"I'm feeling pretty sad about all this."

"All what?"

"This farmhouse. Sarah. Our time together," I said.

"Our time together?"

"A lot of time together."

"Maybe it's better if we stop spending so much."

Sarah Middlemass died taking a nap before dinner. I had gone to wake her. I knocked. I stood beside the bed and shook her shoulders. Her body felt strangely loose and cold. Outside the window stood the continuity of the horizon, the wild beauty of the trees under saffron light, the hazy loom of the barn, the falling snow. I shook her. I called her name. I touched her still-warm skin. With my ear to her mouth, I could not hear her breath. She wore white silk pajamas. A small bedside lamp shone beside her. Her hair was dark and swam with light against her shadowed cheekbones, her rounded nose, and small chin.

I went out of the room, turned left down the hallway, past the twin paintings of mallards, the shelved collection of porcelain dogs. In the kitchen, Donny stir-fried red peppers, Portobello mushrooms, zucchini, chicken. Patti sat at the table with a book. The room smelled like wine. They laughed. They looked at me. And looked. And there must have been something, because we all stood over the bed, her black maul of hair, the white pajamas, the red sheets. Sarah's mouth was open, her eyes closed, her face like a ruined church.

"I think she had a seizure."

"A seizure," I said.

"Donny," Patti said, "do you know what a seizure is?"

"No," he said.

"Neither do I," I said, "not really.

"She said they weren't serious," Donny said. "She laughed."

Donny started vomiting. He held it past the electric lamp on the barn door, back through the snow of the channel, and dropped to his knees on the stairs of the porch. His bare hands touched snow. His vomit was as black and fluid as ink. Patti and I hooked him by the underarms and took him to the bathroom. Patti held his head over the toilet. Her white fingers striped his dark hair. I kept telling Donny that he'd be okay. He gurgled and heaved. Leaning against the sink, I turned the sink tap and ran the water. Patti flushed the toilet twice. I kept thinking his stomach must have emptied. As though she thought he would find it comforting, Patti told Donny that the vomiting was psychosomatic. He wiped his face with the rear of his hand, then heaved again. Patti wiped Donny's forehead with a few sheets of toilet paper. He put his hands on his knees. The veins of his neck stood out. He panted, held his stomach. Patti held his burled hair; I touched his shoulder.

I reimagined the odd pageantry of the three of us traveling the channel through the snow: every snowflake hitting us with weight; Patti putting each foot before her with perfect symmetry; me stumbling beneath the wind and catching myself with both hands; Donny falling to his knees. In the bathroom, amid the retching sound, I looked at myself in the mirror. Behind me lay the reflection of the window. Behind the window, the reflection of the snow.

"Patti," I said.

"What do you have to say?"

"In bed, you asked—"

"I know what I asked."

"I wanted to say—"

"I don't care what you want to say."

"Okay," I said, "I won't say it."

SARAH'S BLUE-GRAY COFFIN hung suspended over the grave. Mourners gathered in a fifty square-foot area plowed of snow. Overhead, thin light shone through a gap in the clouds. Gladiolas, white daisies, and lilies surrounded the hole in the ground. A thin woman in black dropped her scarf. A man waved his arms and spoke. The ends of the dropped scarf flapped as it fell.

This was a cemetery like most, composed of hills and trees and stone. Around me, people were crying into handkerchiefs. Among the semi-circle of people, I stood opposite Patti and Donny. Donny's face looked too white; his suit, exposing ankle and wrist, too small; his yellow tie too bright. Next to him, Patti wore a blond-colored overcoat, tight at the waist. The thin woman, having recovered her scarf, used it to wipe her eyes. Donny held his sides, his cheeks red, his eyes closed, his face wet. Behind the bluish coffin lay a steep hill, columns rising from the snow, the intermittent collapse of snow from the branches of elms, the sun. Was Sarah still frozen? People died, and what was left? Wind in settling gusts, like aborted exhalations. A burial in snow. Particulate dirt in the air curving gracefully in the light. Dust moving back and forth with the pressures of my breath. A series of people spoke, and the land—the sharp, snowy hills; the orchestrated trees; the names chiseled on stone—was shaped by the sound.

The toes of my galoshes were visible past the hem of my overcoat. My hands were covered with worsted mittens. Neither Patti nor I cried. But Donny touched his face with his fingers. The sun shone on all of us. The thin woman's black scarf had fallen again, this time at Patti's feet in the snow. I looked at Patti: her whitewashed skin, her sun-white face, the breaths of wind nattering the tail of her coat—she looked like a bright winged thing.

"I can't shake it," Patti said.

"None of us can," I said.

"All of us standing above her," she said.

"I remember."

"The light from the lantern."

"I know."

"Our mouths. The cold. The ghost of our breath."

When the snow had melted, the funeral had ended, and Sarah's body was secreted beneath earth, Donny, Patti and I went into our separate lives. We barely saw one another. We rarely found occasion to call. But then, when chance brought us together, we sat with the ease and familiarity of family, and drank too many gin and tonics, and spoke of how often we still felt stuck in that farmhouse. Where the lantern on the barn door lightly glowed. Where we went out after supper, stopping halfway to the barn. Where we watched the roiling clouds, the heavy snowfall, the small avalanches on the roof of the barn, the windy cyclones of snow. Where we slipped forward. We touched the icy sides of the channel with our hands. We looked up. We waited for the sky to clear, and the stars to move like darting birds.

The Inconvenience of the Wings

Dominick Clark Sawyer, my father, told me that my mother had been eaten by birds. He tugged on his bottom lip, and then adjusted his wire-rim glasses. I remember we stood in the shallows of the pond behind our house. Our feet were bare. Like the sandpiper across the water, I balanced on one leg. I'd scratched myself on blackberry thorns and blood smeared my calves. The sun was nearly sunk. My father held a kerosene lantern.

"Eaten," he said, "by birds."

"How long ago?" I asked.

"Fourteen years," he said. "You were two."

My father's head nodded sorrowfully. He couldn't believe it either. I remember how he had rolled the cuffs of the legs on my overalls, and then on his trousers. I remember his smell as a meld of oil and woodsmoke. His chin as darkened by whiskers. His voice as faint and whispery.

"What kind of birds?" I asked.

"All kinds," he said. "Carrion feeders."

"Vultures you mean?"

"Sure, vultures. There was a blue jay. A sparrow."

We remember our lives slowly. Memories don't come all at once. Revelation, my father said, is like a funeral procession. The order within the procession tells a story of its own. There's no point to rushing. You need quiet and patience.

A ghost lived in our house, and our house sat by a pond. Our pond didn't hold a single living creature. Dad and I fished there, but our lures weren't alluring. Our bobbers never sunk under. The reflections of the beech trees on the surface were unrippled and leeched of color. The water spoke of what it was to be dead. It was flat, still, and empty; yet on its cold surface it wore our lifeless image.

I remember my father saying how there were things—like the passage of light and the sweep of the past—that we would fail to explain. I remember how anger in my father's voice sounded like sadness. How the air smelled of rot and mildew. How, in the house by the pond, the call of the marsh hawk announced the ghost's coming.

As I sat on a stool peeling sweet potatoes, she blew into the kitchen like wind. The hair on my and my father's necks and backs rose.

"You feel that?" Dad asked. I did. The overhead light began flickering. The marsh hawk screamed loud and high. The moon rose in the window; my father grasped the counter top; I squeezed a sweet potato into pulp. But then the light quit flashing, and the marsh hawk quieted, leaving only the rasp of our breathing. We didn't say anything. We barely looked at one another. Dad pulled a saucepan from the cupboard. We drank mugs of warmed milk, and I went to bed.

In the morning, my father put slices of rye bread in the toaster oven. He wore his red pajamas. He touched my shoulder as he went for the butter.

"Can I tell you something?" I asked.

"Sure," he said.

Last night, I told my father, I'd dreamed of someone dark and hairy holding my face underwater. Bubbles had escaped my nose and mouth. Water rushed. Lungs filled with liquid. I'd seen the shadowed silt of the pond bottom. The drift of my small body.

"Jesus," Dad said, "bad dream." He pushed his glasses up on the bridge of his nose. He broke brown eggs into a skillet. At midnight while I slept, Dad said, the saltshaker rose off the kitchen table and hovered in the air. "You should of seen it," Dad said. "It was something." I nodded. He pulled strips of bacon and tossed them in the pan. "You want orange juice?" he asked.

"Sure," I said.

"Let's call her Ruth," said Dad, "our ghost."

"Mom's middle name?"

"Why not?" Even spirits, Dad told me, needed names. He said that sometimes events coalesced in unthinkable ways. When Dad thought I wasn't looking, he swiped his finger across the dusty cupboard shelf and put his finger in his mouth. The pond, visible outside the window, lay flat as glass. Light filtered through our sheer curtains and shone on the table. I stared at the tabletop.

"Look it here, Dad," I said. "You see this?"

"Yeah," Dad said, "I know. The ghost can write."

The bacon fat crackled. Outside, morning fog receded across the grass. Scrolls of salt spelled words on the table. I touched a line with my finger.

Woodshed, read the words in salt, *birdcall, bone.*

I REMEMBER other things, too:

A flock of geese settling to rest on our pond.

The downy touch of my neighbor, Rosa Bellah's, hands.

The list of ghost words we pinned to the corkboard in my room.

The carved bone of a face that could have been my mother's. Yet wasn't.

A goose biting my finger.

Ruth writing *sylphine* and *rallentando* in salt. Then *throttle, ax handle, nail.*

Visiting the County Library.

Looking up *sylphine* in the dictionary.

I REMEMBER THE CALL of the whippoorwill as Rosa Bellah's mama tried to beat Rosa. At dusk, bolstered by whiskey, Rosa Bellah's mama, in a nightgown, came out on to her porch. Rosa, her skin pale as light, sat next to me in the dirt under the white spruce. Our arms just touched. "Rosa," her mama called from the porch, "You with that boy, King?" Rosa's mama's spectacles were thick as plate glass.

Rosa and her mama lived two lots over, with nearly an acre between us. Their yard held heaps of junk. An overturned wheelbarrow, a rusted sleigh, a pile of tires, a mess of rotting boards.

Rosa's mama liked to toss kitchen utensils. We knew the hierarchy of peril. She whipped a spatula toward us. "Rosa." her mama called, "Get in out of the dark." The whole thing could have been funny, but it wasn't.

"Mama," Rosa yelled, "Calm down." Rosa's mama heaved the crockpot. It landed heavy in the mud. Touching the veiny inside of Rosa's arm, I could feel her heart.

"Don't say nothing," Rosa said. She rolled onto her side, and poked me in the sternum. "Your pop's twice as batty as mama."

"I wasn't saying anything."

"I saw him eating dust."

"Dust?"

"That's right," Rosa said. "Dust." The pepper mill landed between us.

When night settled in, Rosa crept up to plead with her mama. Retreating to the house, I watched with my father from the window, training my flashlight at Rosa's mama on the porch or at Rosa under the white spruce. Rosa's mama tossed the cheese grater, the pasta press, the toaster. Stumbling in her nightgown, hair like a tangle of roots, brandishing the colander, she screamed at Rosa about beating out the darkness, like one beats dust from a rug.

There's a lot I can't remember:

The scent of a red pine.

My first four or five years. Really, I'm not sure how many years I can't remember.

Whether my father was near-sighted or far.

The taste of the pond's water.

Where Rosa Bellah and I stood when she cupped my chin in her hand, looked me in the eyes, and spoke of my father. "He's fucked," she said. "The man eats dust."

The heft of a dead goose.

The depth of my father's boot prints.

Silence. Or emptiness. Or my mother. Can we remember absence?

Or the turkey vultures tugging on strings of vein or fat from my mother's thigh, like robins pulling on worms.

I remember sitting on the roof of our house by the pond. The binoculars rested in my hands. I trained my view on Rosa's lighted window. The room lay empty, all yellow walls.

Twilight was a boring time. An intervening moment where things settled. A dimly lit pause. *Woodshed*, I thought, *birdcall, bone.* I turned the binoculars on the silhouette of a whitethroat that sung from a stand of firs. I answered. A whippoorwill, hunting mosquitoes by the pond, gave the cry that gave the bird its name. My answer was nearly indistinguishable.

I slid down the drainpipe and lugged the dictionary, the list of ghost words, and a flashlight back up.

Pulling shingles from the roof, I side-armed them into the pond. Maybe Ruth was speaking in the only way she knew. What did I know of talking with those beyond the grave? Maybe the grammar was different. What could I know of ghostly syntax? Maybe spilling a single word in salt was an act that left exhaustion in its wake.

24

I remember Rosa Bellah without her top, lying next to me in the tent. The night thickened with low-lying clouds. I remember the way the tent rustled as we moved: the feel of my palm on her belly, the thin gloss of skin, the soft smell of glycerin, the way she twitched beneath my hands.

"You remember anything about your mom?" she asked. Just now, I said, I wasn't sure I remembered how to shrug my pants off.

"About your mom, though. Really."

"Don't think so."

There was a lot of fumbling with buttons. I remember Rosa's tongue. I remember biting the folded skin of her stomach. I remember her mouth.

Since we were small we'd heard from Rosa's mama how maybe my mother had run off with a finer specimen of manhood than my father. A constable, or a pig farmer. In the tent, Rosa turned on the flashlight. She said her mama had been reading the tea leaves, trying to ferret my mother's whereabouts. It wasn't good, Rosa said, this new reading. The tea had turned dark red. Rosa's mama's hands had shook. She broke a china cup. She couldn't see much, Rosa's mama had said, except that my mother was dead.

"Sorry," Rosa said. Her fingers fluttered against my cheek. Her skin pulsed underneath my hands. "I'm not dead," said Rosa.

"Prove it," I said.

I remember her pushing her mouth against mine as the tent walls undulated with wind, and we tore at each other's skins like each wanted the other's for his own. Outside, red warblers trilled, and we, in our own fashion, called back.

Boot, I read in salt, *pinkroot, braid.*

I remember winter. Sitting in the rocker. My father, in his hunting jacket, flooding inside. The wave of cold. The smell of gunpowder. Two geese.

The pond's frozen over, he said. Solid, he said, maybe Ruth drowned there in the pond. He hung his coat on the back of a chair. Before she was a ghost, he said. My father stamped his boots, and then laid them to dry beside the fire. I'll make spiced cider, he said, want some? He sat on the floor, peeled off wet socks. He shivered. Jesus, he said, imagine Ruth. Still there, he said. Frozen under ice.

I remember my father saying that we are manifestations of dust.

I remember practicing birdcalls, weaving through the aspens, following the tapping of the pileated woodpeckers, and stumbling across the wood-shed. Crows scattered as I approached. The wood had rotted soft. It crumbled beneath my hands like earth. Moss covered the stacks. Mushrooms bloomed. The woodshed's roof had fallen in. I pushed split wood about with my foot. Beside the stacks lay a pair of men's workboots, one upright, and one overturned. In the upright boot, lay a leather sack. In the sack was a braid of dark hair.

Dust, I remember reading, *boning knife, red pine.*

I REMEMBER finding the carcass of a rooster, its belly scratched open. Intestines strewn across yellow grass.

The herringbone stitch on the hem of Rosa Bellah's blue dress.

The canoe my father gave me for Christmas.

Asking Rosa Bellah what she thought about her mother throwing things at her in the night. She didn't know, she said, she tried not to think about it.

My father knuckling his eyes, saying that the things we see aren't true. And the things we don't see, are.

My father running his forefinger along the plane of the bookshelf, pinching dust, raising it to his mouth.

Ruth writing, *Do, re, mi, fa, sol, la, ti, do*, on the bathroom floor. In pepper. We were looking after Rosa Bellah's hound, Sheba. She snuffed the pepper and sneezed. We laughed hard, Dad and me, the back-thumping kind of hee-haw that doesn't come much. We watched the sniff, the face wrinkle, the jump of the nose, the wobble of the head at the intake of air, and then the series of wet dog sneezes. Sheba backed off a few feet, half frightened. She put her nose low to the ground, shuffled forward, sniffed again.

Finding salt scrolled on our floor. *Rimrock, pinkroot, ring.*

BEHIND THE POND, I found a red pine strung with decayed rope. Near the trunk, I remember, lay a broken clay pot of pinkroot flowers. The earth rose steeply here and on the upper portion of the slope lay the rimrock. *Rimrock. Pinkroot. Ring.* My fingers tingled as with cold. What had happened to Ruth? I climbed the rimrock, scoured through the dirt and fist-sized stones, and came upon a rotten ax handle, rust eaten manacles, a torn sack of roofing nails. Kicking at loose rocks, I uncovered three thin, white lengths of bone, none longer than an inch. And then a silver ring.

I REMEMBER how in the morning Rosa Bellah's mother, eyes bound by dark circles and voice husky from smoke, read tea leaves. Rosa tugged me inside. The porch steps bowed as we climbed. I followed because I didn't want to let go of Rosa's hand. The parlor was dark. All the house curtains, purple but sun-faded, were drawn. The moist air held a chill. Water stains covered the ceiling. The air hung with mildew.

Rosa's mama sat in a chair near a table. She poured tea. When Rosa's mama looked up from the cup, her wide, slack face made her look like she was sleepwalking. "Any man who eats dust will soon die," she said. She slurred her words. She swished the tea in the china. Her watery eyes held me a long time. "Your father," she said, "killed."

FINGER, I read in salt, *manacle, throat.*

I REMEMBER how, looking for duct tape in my father's tackle box, I found a boning knife. The handle darkened; the blade deeply notched. I put it back. I shivered. Trotting across our yard, I dove into the pond and let myself settle to the bottom. Driving my palms into silt, I felt for bones. I wouldn't return to the surface until I found them. My hands closed around soft branches, round stones, tin cans. My lungs tore my insides. Bubbles escaped my mouth and rose toward the light on the surface. Turning my head upward, I saw myself as a woman in manacles, a woman tied to a red pine, a woman beaten with an ax handle. Holding my breath became worse than breathing water. I opened my mouth; let it rush in; surrendered and became Ruth: my skull cracked by ax handle, tied to the red pine, ring finger carved off with a boning knife. My wrist pierced with a roofing nail. Seizures wracked my body and then I was free, crawling toward the light shining off the surface of the pond, touching the skin of the water, watching the cloud of blood spread from my hands. Then the yank of my braid, the give of the scalp, the tearing and screaming, and the fingers at my throat, holding my head beneath water. Holding my head still as my limbs flailed.

And as my body kicked upward from the pond bottom, broke the surface, and breathed in the light, I saw the face that looked back into mine as I drowned.

UNDER THE WHITE SPRUCE, I remember Rosa and me.

"I don't think he did it," I said.

"Sure he did."

"But he's my dad. And he's pretty good."

"What kind of people you think do bad things?"

I REMEMBER my father showing me how to gut fish, how to scale them, string them by the gills. How to identify trout, perch, bluegill. How to make lures, to fish in jetties and hollows, to toss the guts on the stones for the circle of crows. I remember him carrying me home, trail worn and blistered, over hills.

I asked my father as directly as I could. We were fishing the Kishwaukee River. I asked like this: "Dad, you ever kill anybody?"

The banks of the Kishwaukee rolled with gentle hills. The rains had made the river fierce. Whitewater crashed above sunken boulders. The air, damp and hot, shimmered under the sun. Steam rose from our damp boots.

"Wasn't me," Dad said. He took of his glasses, wiped them on his shirt.

"Wasn't you what?"

"All flesh is grass," Dad said. His eyes were wide and wet. He fidgeted with his pole.

"Alright then," I said.

We tossed our lines out in hopes of perch or trout. Our hooks kept snagging.

"Why's our ghost named Ruth?" I asked.

"Your mother's middle name. You know that." Dad's feet moved as though they wanted to take him elsewhere. His lips were thin.

"I know that."

"Why'd you ask then?" Dad's eyes rested on the water.

"Why'd you name the ghost after *mom*?" The lines from both of our poles were caught in the middle of the river. We pulled. The poles bowed.

"Better clear this snag," my father said. He looked straight at me, and then he jumped in.

"Shit," I said. I stood in the shallows, my legs smeared with mud. My father went under and resurfaced in the deep.

"My clothes are damn heavy," he called. The river whipped him downstream; he breaststroked toward the snag, rather than the bank. I remember the sight of his strong arms pistoning through the air and water, the flash of awe and indignation on his face at a current stronger than him, the gleam of droplets scattering under the sun.

There's more I don't remember:

My father saying, "Listen here, King, I done something wrong."

Me asking, "What?"

And my father telling me.

I REMEMBER my father being borne on the flood. The flail toward the surface. The holding of breath, the underwater gasp, the wash of lungs. I remember the limpness of body flowing around stones, rising toward the surface, toward the brown-yellow light, only to be swept toward the silt and rock bottom. To slow here, to catch against a tire, against stone, against the tongues of yellow-green weeds. Hand-sized perch scattered at his approach. His shorts caught on a branch and he hung there, one leg rising to break the surface, as the current pressed and tickled and worried the wire-rimmed glasses from his face, the few bubbles from his mouth, and then the shorts tore and he flowed. Above him, the skin of the water undulated with light. One hand, dragging along the river bottom, raised a slowly expanding trail of silt. Branches and leaves rode the currents. Shafts of light refracted at odd angles. The water slowed as the base of the river widened; he floated under a wharf, past the pilings. His body slowly rotated, facing up toward the sun-mottled surface—the minnows silvered by slants of light—and the marsh heron, its whoosh and flap silenced by depth, blurred across the skin. My father's body gently rose toward the sweep and grace of distorted wings.

River, I read in salt, *father, sound.*

I REMEMBER the shine of lights on water. Unfamiliar voices calling my father's name. Sturdy men in clothing that repelled water. Seal-like men in the depths. Search lights. Silver-hulled motorboats; the thunder and wind of a helicopter. My legs hung off the dock. Searchlights dove into water. *Dominick*, the men in boats called, *Dominick*! But this was no longer my father's name.

Later, standing in these shallows, I'll call birds. I'll be overwhelmed by visions of water. The images will come at me doubled up and overlaid. I'll remember standing, pants rolled high, in the fringes of the pond by the house or in the edgewaters of the Kishwaukee River. My skin smeared with dirt or blood. My toes curled in mud or silt. The water lapping at my calves. And with the sweep of remembrance will come the resurrection of a hundred other times I'd hooted and whistled and cupped my hands, almost as in prayer, before my lips.

In this place, I'll have many mouths. All these cries echo across the water. I call them: the whitethroats, the hoot owls and whippoorwills, the robins and finches, the hawks and crows, the warblers, the woodpeckers, the marsh herons. Raising all my faces skyward and working my many lungs, I call them, and then call them again. And, carrying both promise and pestilence, they come.

The Archimedes Palimpsest

Our lives recall the textual. For one winter of my adult life, my father and I lived in a farmhouse in Boone County, Illinois. This was 1999. My father, Asel Poole, was dying of lymphoma. My wife and I had separated. The earth wintered; the air turned sharp with cold; the fields stretched expansively in white. My father viewed the season as a metaphor for our condition. Physically, much of the time he seemed to get along fine. He tended to conceive of any passing symptom of his lymphoma as prophetic. I recall a fit of coughing as he stood near the woodstove. He wore longjohns. His white beard swept his face. His angled face was mine, only at a distance that made it less familiar. My father coughed, bent over, touched the wood floor with one hand.

Out the window, a lone dark-red bird curved over our lake. When steadying my father, my fingers—in the hollows of his elbow and armpit—caught on lymph nodes the size of concord grapes. In the main room, I sat my father on a rocking chair beside the blackened-iron woodstove. Across from him, on the couch, I listened to the wheeze in his chest ebb, watched the flush of his cheeks fade, the breathing steady, the rigid musculature relax. The woodstove's round chimney pipe leaked smoke from multiple ruptures. Heavy snow bedecked the roof. Three-foot icicles hung from the gutters. Under wind, the branches of the elm by the lake soundlessly rattled. The snow lay thick outside; the fields were shielded in white. The lake, a rough circle, was slowly freezing beneath the gray-blue sky. Farmhouses lumped in the distance. Smoke trailed from three or four chimneys and then, beyond them, lay the curve of the earth.

My father looked at the bluish ice on the lake, the fields of snow, the barren sky. The sunlight's odd glimmer lightened his eyes.

Near the woodstove, beneath a plant light, my father grew a marmalade tree. He plucked dead leaves, watered on Tuesdays, fertilized the soil. He lit the tree with a ground light that cast shadows of the tree's large leaves and egg-shaped fruit against the wall. He stared into the tree.

"You okay, dad?" I said. "I'll water the tree." I asked my father how he was feeling too frequently, and my question caused a tightening of lips and of brow.

"You don't know a thing about it," he said.

"I can water a tree."

My father sat in the rocker near the woodstove. Of the split logs piled alongside the stove, he preferred the worm-eaten, feeling with his palms the hieroglyphic furrows. He added a log to the fire. Within the vagaries of foliation or combustion—the budding leaves on the marmalade tree, the bloom of flame on worm-eaten wood—my father seemed fascinated with his role, though his role was as small as the hand that fed the marmalade tree, the fingers that held the match to wood. He studied the brachiation of veins in fallen leaves and the coloration of ash in the woodstove as though within them remained a record of his hand.

Adding two logs to the fire, my father glanced at me. I stripped off my vest. He added another log.

"You out to start us on fire?" I said.

He put on his wool vest, his hunting jacket, a scarf and cap, knee-high boots. By the door he stopped, turned toward me. Hanging flat beneath his hat, his long, dark hair framed his face.

"What're you thinking?" he said.

"My wife."

"What about?" he said.

"The heart is a deep lake, she said."

"She said that?" My father shook his head, stomped his feet. "That's not bad."

He opened the door and went outside. He put a lawn chair in the snow beneath the elm on the hill. The half-frozen lake stretched behind him. There he wrote in a notebook. Above him, the snow-laden elm hung like an umbrella in white. Earlier, he had pulled books from the attic—Updike's *The Music School*; Nabokov's *Details of a Sunset*; Archimedes' *The Works of Archimedes*—and left them on the kitchen table beside two notebooks. And I—who never read then, who hadn't used a pen but to sign a check since my school days—picked up the books, felt their covers with my fingertips, and sat watching the silhouette of my father and his pencil against the hill, the sun setting on the lake behind him, the endless run of white cornfield.

Years later I would read everything he had left behind.

Outside, as my father opened a notebook to write, my tear ducts threatened to loosen, the valves of my heart to open wide. As he wrote, his pen seemed to scrape against the underside of my skin. And as, beneath the elm, my father lifted his hand before his mouth to silently cough, I sensed the duration of that winter, blank as a page, and understood at least one meaning of lymphoma, and, attending this, the likelihood of my father dying with the end of the millennium.

My father had left a pen on the edge of the kitchen table. I opened a notebook and wrote. What I wrote, in my father's notebook, beside my father's lightly penciled words, summoned small memories—my father, beardless, holding a football before me; my wife, reddish hair sectioning her face, asleep in our bed; my father placing a pear before me on a plate; her smooth thigh against mine; my father, in overalls, reading to me as I sat on his lap—and beneath me I sensed, like a text, my father's form and voice, and then distantly, beneath them, deeper like music whose source was untraceable, other more heavenly bodies.

Prior to his death in 212 BC, Archimedes, the Greek thinker and mathematician, penned his theories onto papyrus scrolls. Many of the treatises he wrote, among them *On Floating Bodies* and *The Method*, remained lost until 1907. The treatise, *On Floating Bodies*, gave the weight of a body immersed in fluid. *The Method* dealt, in part, with infinite sums.

Archimedes' theories survived centuries by being copied from scroll to scroll. Not until the tenth century were the treatises bound into book form. The book's cover was constructed of wood; the leaves made of the skins of sheep and goats. In the twelfth century, in the city of Constantinople, a scribe dismantled the Archimedes manuscript and imperfectly rubbed out the text. He cut the leaves in half, turned them ninety degrees, ruled new lines, and copied a new text onto the surface. So the Archimedes manuscript became a palimpsest, a text overwritten by another text.

Imagine how, over the accumulation of years, the leaves of skin must have burned, moldered and torn. Imagine the darkening of age. Imagine how turning each heavy page turned two pages of text, the obvious and the embedded.

Our lives have been similarly inscribed. On the top lies the text that we've written, a series of instructions on how to stand in a shower without slipping, how to angle a razor against the skin of the cheek, how to wear a jacket that lends our shoulders an illusion of breadth, how to starch and iron a button-down, how to tie a half Windsor, how to lower our voices to sound calm, how to touch a woman's skin—or a father's—lightly with our own.

Beneath the first physical impression lies the transmundane.

As I sat watching my father write beneath the elm, I took off my jacket. Beneath the threadbare jacket, I wore a blue undershirt, printed with a gray whale, that belonged to my father. Come to recall, my wife bought me the pinstriped boxers I wore beneath my pants. Beneath the flowered wallpaper of the farmhouse, at the junctures of planes where the wallpaper peeled, a faded red paint was exposed. Behind the cornices of wrinkles on my forehead, beside my mouth—accumulating year by year and likening my image to my father's—there still lay a boy's unlined face. Beneath my skin lay muscle, sinew, bone. And beneath that lay the heart, struggling to rush the blood inside me.

In 1204, the city that housed the Archimedes Palimpsest, Constantinople, suffered under the fourth Crusade. Instead of rushing to the Holy Land, the Crusaders stopped to loot and burn. Plumes of fire consumed the city. Soot obscured the sky. Blood washed the ancient streets. The Archimedes Palimpsest survived.

On the night of the coughing fit, my father sat up sweating. His intestines, he said, were a leviathan twisting inside him. I held his shoulders as he emptied his stomach into the toilet. He shook with a great fever. I wiped the beaded sweat from his head with toilet paper. The bathroom lights reflected off the white tile. The room smelled acrid and sweet.

My father heaved and sweat. I held his hair from his head.

"Mormons called today," he said. His breathing was labored. His skin damp. His eyes dark.

"You okay, dad?"

"Quoted at me."

"Ready to try the bed?"

"'When the waves of death encompassed me,' the Mormons said, 'when the torrents of destruction overwhelmed me…I called upon the Lord… and he sent from on high, he took me, he drew me out of many waters.'"

The Archimedes manuscript, overwritten, became a religious text called the Euchologion. The Euchologion would supply monks and priest with the rituals believed necessary for salvation. Beneath the Euchologion lay Archimedes' treatises on the weight of a body in water, on the infinity of sums. The word *palimpsest* comes from the Latin *palimpsestus* meaning scraped or rubbed again.

In the morning beneath the elm tree, where I dragged a kitchen chair to write in my father's notebook, I found my father had written a variation on his name in the snow. Above, the sun worked on obviating the night. Ice cracked and fell from the branches of the elm. My father: Asel Poole. In the snow my father had left out the vowels. SLPL.

Only now does it occur to me: this was a tetragrammaton. Tetragrammaton: the four consonants of the ancient Hebrew name for God, often transliterated as JHVH. The name of God was once considered too sacred to be spoken aloud. Why was the name too sacred? Maybe the tetragrammaton, those four consonants with their vowels excised, acknowledged our inability to see God, chief representative of the infinite, in his entirety. I remember looking at those four letters in the snow. SLPL. As I sat beneath the elm, looking at the series of letters in the snow and even, after a moment, hearing my father's footsteps approach behind me, I could not imagine my father whole.

My father broke a hole in the thin ice with his cane. "We ought to leap in," he said. "But too cold." He stared at the slow lap of water against air. Wind blew streamers of hair across his face. His lips were dry and cracked.

"See here," he said. He stirred the surface with the point of his cane. The clouds swirled above us. I couldn't know if I saw what my father did. What I thought then for the first time, gazing through the hole in the ice, was this: what we knew as the division between water and air was, in a manner of speaking, the observable collision between two infinities.

As a sacred text, the Archimedes Palimpsest was cared for in the Holy Land. By the sixteenth century, the manuscript was kept at the Greek Orthodox Monastery of Mar Saba. The monastery lay in the Judean desert, between Bethlehem and the Dead Sea, in the wilderness where Christ wandered for forty days. The Mar Saba Monastery had a reputation for hospitality. The Euchologion was essential to daily life, containing exorcisms for unclean spirits and prayers for the sick. As a religious text, the palimpsest was used at Mar Saba for four hundred years.

The monastery was a fortress.

At night the dim walls off the farmhouse hulked around my father and me. The plant light lit the marmalade tree. Snow silently fell outside the windows. Flakes flattened themselves against the glass and melted. Distant lights intermittently winked out. The heavy smell of wood smoke and the haze in the room blurred the image of my father reclining in the chair across from me. She called—my wife. Her voice: soft, diffuse, and approachable, like the flannel sheet I'd wrapped around me.

"You okay?" she said.

"Fine, I'd say."

"How's your father?"

I looked at him. The sunken placidity of skin. The loss of mass. The shadows blooming under each eye. The pain taut on his lips. My father looked back at me, raised his drink in cheers.

"Good," I said. "He's good."

"Any of this true?" she said. We'd spent a lot of time together.

"Well," I said, "we've got our share of trouble."

"How much?"

"It's hard to measure."

We, my father and I, sat there growing older and dying. Across the phone line, I heard nothing but my wife's breathing. The fire cracked in the woodstove. For a moment, the moon lit the floor in panes. We, my wife and I, struggled to find words to say to each other.

"What do you feel about us?" I said.

"Not much."

"No?"

"That's what I called to say," she said. "I needed you to know. I don't feel much."

In the early nineteenth century, the Archimedes Palimpsest traveled from the Monastery of Mar Saba to the library of the Greek Patriarch in old Jerusalem, and from there passed among religious hands. Likely, the manuscript traveled to the Church of the Holy Sepulchre. The Church of the Holy Sepulchre housed the Rock of Golgotha, the site of Christ's crucifixion, and of his resurrection.

In bed, wrapped in blue woolen blankets, my father's body assumed alphabetic shapes. I sat in the cane rocking chair and watched over his breathing. He breathed quite shallowly, stretched, lengthened into an *I*. This *I* stood for him. Or for me. Or was it the first letter in *ice*? He twisted and curled into a *C*. This might be the first *C* in *calculus*. Or in *cancer*. Or maybe not a *C*, but a crescent or curve, the half-grin of the moon. With arms thrown out to his sides, he formed a *T*. Perhaps not a *T*, but a cross; not a cross but a crucifix. Did our bodies belong to us? Were we all Christs? His breathing quickened, becoming almost a pant. Twisting his two arms at angles, my father's body formed a *Y*. This was a question. My father asked a question. Did I? Studiously, I wrote the letters down, treated them as though they might betray some meaning. I scrambled and unscrambled them. The only possibilities I considered came in the English language—little did I know of Greek or Latin. What possibilities might my father's body have taken if I had known the alphabets of the languages embedded beneath my own?

In 1907, at the Metochion in Constantinople, a Danish philologist named Johan Heiburg photographed each page of the Archimedes Palimpsest and transcribed it with a magnifying glass. Eventually, Heiburg realized that the imbedded manuscript was an unknown work by Archimedes.

In 1999, at the farmhouse in Illinois, my father tossed a stone through a hole in the ice of a pond. I watched from the window. The water rippled in concentric circles.

The chief discovery in the Palimpsest was *The Method*. In *The Method*, Archimedes combined pure math and an earthly consideration of shape, the abstract and the worldly, the infinite and the finite. By placing segments of geometrical objects on a scale, he measured the area and volume of the objects. Then Archimedes performed infinite sums, calculating the volume of a sphere as the infinite sum of the circles by which it was formed.

Concentric circles upon the surface of water widen slowly and fade. My father's life has a volume that I cannot measure. The space that another occupies within us refuses to be defined. The Greek word *apeiron* means without boundary. Apeirophobia, a term with Greek roots, means to fear the infinite. Aristotle acknowledged that the counting numbers (one, two, three, four, five, and so on) could be *theoretically* infinite, because, counting endlessly, we fail to reach any highest number. Yet Aristotle believed the counting numbers could not be *actually* infinite, because it is impossible to imagine the entire set of counting numbers as a finished thing, as whole.

The snow engulfed the farmhouse, white and limitless. Our fortress of warmth. My father and I. This life.

The Roman emperor Marcus Aurelius named infinity as a fathomless gulf, into which all things vanish. Archimedes, in the palimpsest, added an infinite number of circles until he found a single definable sphere.

Inside, my father made me lunch. He set the chipped stoneware on the table. Lay out the silver. Filled water glasses.

"You hungrier than you look?" he said. We ate split-pea soup with ham hock, and cornbread. Our spoons scraped, high-pitched, against the bottoms of our bowls. My father feathered his beard with his fingers. His eyes glinted narrowly. Head down, he glanced at me sideways.

"What say we take a swim in the lake?" he said.

"Nuts," I said.

"Come on and give me a watch then."

Next to the lake, we stood. We shivered. Sunlight reflected off the ice and warmed the air. In 214 BC when Marcellus and his Roman army invaded Syracuse they were thwarted by the enormous curved mirrors that Archimedes had placed on top of the city's walls. The sun's rays, reflected from the mirrors, set the ships' sails on fire.

In a steel barrel, my father and I put the notebooks to match. It was his idea. We rolled the barrel out near the lake. We slung the notebooks inside, and my father lit the fire. Then he began to strip down. He stood in the snow on the edge of the lake in his boxer shorts. I pulled the collar of my jacket tight; rubbed my hands together before the flames.

There was no beach. Beneath our feet and the snow lay stone. Just before us, off the stone ledge and through the hole in the thin ice, the lake was six feet deep. A pair of dark-red birds arched over the sky. The lake bottom looked etched with currents. The sun wrote in light across the water. My father bent to touch the surface.

Imagine yourself, cold with fear, at the first touch of water. Imagine this lake. The snowfields. The blue-gray of ice. The jagged hole my father had broken. The freezing touch of water against your fingers reminding you that you don't exist without limits.

Snow, so fine that we could not feel it on our skin, drifted from clouds sheer enough to reveal the sun. Fire flickered over the lip of the barrel. My father slipped into the water. There was no sound. No waves. Imagine that bit of warmth, the infinite sum of heat, that contains you. Imagine being wrapped in fingers of cold. Imagine being whispered to by the weight of ice.

I stood above my father. There was a quiet then, which I want to capture here. The quiet just before a moment of unmeasured importance, when you are sitting, tense with this potential energy, in a chair before a closed window and watching a clouded, soundless outdoors.

I looked out upon the place that I was. On the light streaming behind the thin clouds, on the reaching branches of the elm, the run of snow, the fields. Then I looked down. At my father, floating underwater: his skin a pale and translucent blue, his eyes as obdurate as night. His hand rising from the water—from the depths of the mystery that cupped us in its palm—clawing at the air, searching either to be pulled out, or, more likely, to pull me in.

Outlaw

WHAT HOOT RAWLEY talked about was the time before we were revisions of ourselves. The late afternoon was unblemished. Heat rose from the heaps of stone beneath us, and willows spotted the base of the gully. Hoot Rawley held a pair of six-guns; he was sixteen years old, cloaked in dust, run with sweat. Soon, Hoot said, we would smell of blood.

"Peckerwood," Montana White said, "Arsehump."

The whine of bullets clove the air. Full-mouthed heifers straggled along a barbed fence. Over a bramble fire, I fried grouse eggs in a skillet. My dog, Royal, lay in the milkweed as I, with a free hand, picked ticks off his neck.

Hoot Rawley hadn't quit talking bull. He was on about what we once were and some such. He spoke of *invisible spectrums, unholy numbers,* and *ad infinitums.* No one paid him any mind. With the rifle, Montana took potshots at prairie dogs and practiced his cursing. He said something about *jabberjaws,* and *windbags,* and *skinbladders full up with piss.* Then, turning in Hoot's direction, Montana spat in an arc. He was whip-thin, almond-skinned. His gaze was steady as a rattler's; his hands undersized and womanish and viper-fast. "You seen that, Buzz?" Montana said, "I cut that dog in half."

"Well yeah, I seen it," I said. I cocked my hat to the left.

"Fuckback," Montana said, "Hossshit."

Horseflies droned among the weeds. The contrail of a jet plane cut the sky in two.

"Towards whom might your foul commentary be aimed?" Hoot asked.

"Damned if I know," said Montana. "Who you reck'n?"

Halved prairie dogs littered the field. Wheel ruts led toward town lights. My El Camino sat beneath a chestnut tree. As I fried eggs, I sung slow songs about love.

"Shitfire," Montana said, "Bumhole." The cast of Montana's squinty eyes and his tone of voice suggested he might have been speaking of Hoot Rawley. Hoot, sitting on a slab of dark granite and still jawing, gave Montana the finger.

These were the rolled hills we haunted in the stillness of our youths before we pointed our father's rifles and six-guns in wayward directions; before I, Buzz Woodhouse, turned myself into a crybaby; before the trail of the dead led backward toward our former selves. This was back before the earth bucked and rolled and the chestnut trees laid themselves flat. Before my Aussie Shepherd, Royal, ceased living in a way that no dog, nor man, ought ever see. Before the rain came down as gasoline. Sweet Hell, that was a whole other time then.

The wind pitched leaves in curlicues. The trickle of running water echoed in the gully. My dog Royal chewed on a rag of prairie dog.

"Look it 'ere, shitsacks," said Montana, "I nabbed sumthin from daddy." Montana White was mean as time and quick with a gun. He had a fondness for nursing animals with incurable diseases, amputating healthy pet limbs, mutilating rabbits. Montana White generally shot to maim. He rifled through his leather satchel. He took out a bottle by the neck. "Whiskey," he said, "and dynamite." He laid two red sticks on a rock.

"Holy moly," I said, "that'll turn the trick." People knew me as thick-middled, pan-faced, and lovesick. My voice held the pitch of an ear ache.

Pollen shone in the air. We passed the bottle and swilled whiskey out of hollowed-out gourds. "Blunderbuss," I said, "ain't this silly. We bought these gourds at the grocery market."

Hoot Rawley stood tall on an outcropping of granite. He wore a buck knife strapped to his thigh, a handkerchief around his neck. Like a bull-horn, Hoot stood narrow at the foot and widened as he rose to the shoulder. His gait was loose but calculated, like sums rounded to the whole number. He was deliberately squint-eyed. He wiped his dry palms on his thighs. He held his gourd of whiskey high.

"I've come," Hoot said, "to speak of serious things." The sun glared behind him. "You and me," said Hoot, "we're out to force this world into atonement. What say we turn to banditry and commence to speak in verse?"

There was a chorus of hows. We were men who wanted to be given answers. We were partial to words of explanation. Hoot, perched up on the rock, looked like a creature out of the desert. My dog Royal nuzzled his boots.

"Git off yer fuckin highhorse," Montana said. He squatted on the ground spinning the chamber of his six-gun.

"We talked of burgling the Texaco," Hoot said. "Our time has come." Hoot Rawley cast his eyes on the sky. He wiped his face with a dusty hand. "You tell me this: Have we seen sorrows that no man ought to have known?"

Sure, we reflected, we had. We raised our gourds and drank a toast.

"Yer damn straight," Montana said. He fired a round through a prairie dog.

We'd all had family pilfered from us. Last year, Montana's younger brother, Junior, got steer kicked and died. Montana liked to say that Junior had gotten off easy. Wasn't but the year before Junior died that, while Montana napped, Montana's daddy diced him and his sister up with a straight razor; his sister never did pull through. I thanked heaven my daddy stewed in prison. Hoot's daddy died liquored up in a boating mishap.

"When we gain infamy," Hoot said, "we must guard against blame being placed on the ill-will of fatherhood."

"Damn it," Montana said, "I blame that shitass for all I can."

"There's a lot that's been taken from us," I said, "I say it's time to take something back." I could feel the blood rise to my face, the heat of fermented courage.

Hoot thrust an arm out and pointed behind us. I swiveled my head toward a gentle hill. Beyond the hill lay a county gas station.

What Hoot Rawley asked was why we had to do this, and what we were thinking, and what might we come to after? Hoot pointed out that we squatted in a gully a mile behind the Texaco that, come nightfall, we figured on knocking off. What made us think we were thieves? Why'd we purchase buck knives and bandanas from the Army Surplus? Why'd we steal my daddy's crowbar, and pry open Montana's daddy's gun cabinet, and pass out guns first come first serve? Hoot wanted to know what had come over us.

"Listen now," I said, "what about *doing unto others* and all that business? Love for our fellow man. What about it being wrong to steal?"

"Here's a question of a higher order," Hoot said. He lay back on a slab of rock and looked drowsy. He blew on the cherry of his cigarette and jabbed it at the sky. "Whatever made us think there might be something wrong with outlawry?"

"Listen, runt," Montana said, "you best quit talkin as such. It ain't fittin."

"How about I say reckon more frequently?"

"Yer shit ain't fit for pissin on," Montana said.

Maybe, under the powerful lull of the whiskey, we nodded off between times, lay back in the high grass and cocked our hats over our eyes. White-tails called from the hill over. Not much could sneak by us. We closed our eyes and laughed about Hoot Rawley saying things like *swindle* and *whitherward, palaver* and *watering hole;* about Montana White's recurring dream of losing himself in undiscovered Illinois deserts and of the heat of the sun and of skinning swine alive; about my fixation on teenage girls with M names like Marilyn, Margo, Melissa, Maggy, Mary—I'd loved them, I sure had, I'd loved them all—and then our hee-hawing and knee-slapping over Hoot Rawley's scratchy baritone getting nearly tearful and sounding off about us being fishermen caught up in our own lines of bullshit and how just at this moment, in the here and now—with the blindness of lowered lids reinforced by his hat's shade—he had the feeling we weren't nothing but words.

We knew we had to do something. Break the mold. Shake things up and set things loose. This could be done, Hoot said. We could do it.

Montana White let loose a holler. "Assjack," he shouted, "Pussywail."

Hoot Rawley stood up, looking as mean as famine and as grim as drought, and turned to face the hill. "Listen," Hoot said, "we ain't meant for cushy times. Fuck these here suburbs."

Montana drew on his cigarette and gestured to the welter of lights on the horizon. "Yer right," he said. "But yer a shitsack."

"We're men of spirit and grit," Hoot said, casting a thumb toward me. "Montana, it's likely you're not."

"Hoot," I said, "there ain't nothing for it. We been called out. Death has fucked with us one too many times." Snaking my arms around Royal's neck, I wrestled him to the ground; he yelped and nipped my wrist.

"Sumbitch," Montana said, "We got to do what's got to be done. Our calling's to kill things." He took to shaking trees and corking crows like they were skeet.

We'd be the first and last of our kind.

"Hey now," I said. The fall of the sun had struck me dumb. "Remind me what we been called out by?"

"Inequity," Hoot said, "and loss. I say fuck the quiet life. There's poetry to be found in misdeeds. Take up your guns."

We piled into my El Camino and drove over the hill. We smoked and drove in silence. From the backseat, Hoot Rawley spoke in warning of the corruption of what we called physics: a muzzle pointed outward had the circumference of a huckleberry, but turned toward you, a musk melon. He demonstrated by pointing a six-gun in my direction. "We're sweet," Hoot said, "but soon we aren't to be."

The Texaco sign loomed above us. The windows of the station faced westward. Beyond the station lay a line of chestnut trees and a pair of Japanese maples. The Japanese maples had red leaves. We rolled the El Camino up to the gas pump and, as our boots stepped onto the pavement and our closing doors concussed simultaneously, we yanked our neckerchiefs up to bridge our noses. Royal jumped out of the El Camino and snuffed at trash. We pulled six-guns. We paced evenly across the cement as though we'd rehearsed.

We kicked the door open and went in. The store consisted of a sea of snack food in four isles, a refrigerator case flush with beer, a single restroom, and the front counter where the clerk stood. We knew this man. He picked at his teeth with a penknife; he had skin tough as rawhide.

"Son of a whore," Montana said, "that's Earl Suggs." Earl Suggs was formed mostly out of potbelly. He was hairless; a mass of lumpen, clay-colored flesh.

"Don't change nothing," I said.

The late-day sun cut in the windows and lit half the floor. Passing clouds caused the room to blink.

Suggs saw us coming; failed to register awe at the sight of our six-guns and neckerchiefs; took a smoke from behind his ear and lit up. "What you want?" said Suggs. "You look dumb in them get-ups." He blew smoke in our direction.

"Well now," I said, "our list of wants might take a spell."

Hoot stood near the register; I lingered near the magazines; Montana covered the door. Each of us trained our guns toward Earl. "We are here," Hoot said, "to make an unlawful withdrawal."

"Withdrawal?" said Earl, "What you talking?" His face screwed up into a map of wrinkles. "You talkin drugs?"

"I may be in need of an interpreter," said Hoot.

"Interpreter? Shit, fella, this here is a gas station." Earl slowed his speech and wrapped his knuckle against the counter at each word. "*A Gas Station.*"

"Yer money, shitass," Montana said, "it's ours now."

"Christ, boy, why didn't you say so?" Suggs' gestured toward Hoot with his cigarette and looked around at all of us through half-lowered lids. Smoke floated in ribbons on the air. "Damn," Suggs said, "What're you in this for?"

"I'm gonna hurt some things," said Montana. "Take another's money." He rifled through the array of lighters on the counter. "Him there," Montana pointed to me. "It's love he's after."

"Love, Illinois," said Earl. "That's a town. Hundred miles south of here."

"I say, man," Hoot said, "we're on the prowl for what we once were."

"Shit, boy," Earl said, "that almost sounds like English."

"It ain't," I said, "no how. Don't listen to a word of it."

"I think the chump's playing dumb," Hoot said. He pushed his six-gun into the crick in the clerk's neck. "You seen our past selves? Don't you lie."

"Never you mind," Montana said. "Put the dough in a sack."

The colors of the wrapped snacks came in every hue. The air smelled of spiced meat and sugar and smoke. Montana White breathed like a bellows.

Earl Suggs manipulated the cash register. "I got eleven dollars, twenty cents. You still need that sack?"

"Go on, chucklehead," I said. I thrust my gun over the magazine rack and hid my body behind. My legs were crossed and my free hand cupped my privates as though I feared wetting myself.

Hoot Rawley hadn't quit drawling on. The rest of us were doing our damnedest to ignore him. He'd worked himself into a lather of sweat. He hawked sputum on the station floor. "I am an agent of periphrais," he said, "of circumlocution. That is to say I like to talk the talk of wise men, my friend, and most cannot make head nor tails of me."

"What say?" Suggs said. "Who the hell you think you is, boy?"

"You know me as the loom of mystery, the dark maw, the perambulation of night. I am an expression of metaphors, a construction of pseudonyms."

"Well," said Earl Suggs, "I ain't good with talk. You got a nickname?"

"My friends call me the seamouth or the invisible choir."

"Hell," Montana said, "no one ain't never called you none of that." He pushed Hoot in the chest with his gun barrel. "Yer pissin me off."

The falling sun crept across the Texaco's floor. Light glared through liquids of unearthly colors. Earl pointed at Montana. "Hang on," he said, "I'll mess my pants if you ain't Monty White's boy. Me and him split a bottle last Sunday."

Montana White seemed to glow from the inside. His face twisted. "Damn straight," he said. "That's me. I'm the one's gonna kill you."

"Son," Earl said, "the cops'll be on you like flies on shit."

"Shit damn," I said, "it's a bust." Outside, sunlight gleamed off the polished steel of the twin gas pumps.

"You there," Earl said, "over by the skin pictures. That Buzz Woodhouse?"

"Nuthin fer it," Montana said, "I get to shoot him now." Montana cocked his gun.

"Listen, Suggs," Hoot said, "we've taken on new aspects. We ain't the men we used to be. But Montana, you ain't shooting Earl Suggs."

Montana grabbed Earl Suggs by the shoulder, quick-hauled him across the countertop and onto the tiled floor, put a knee to his chest, and a six-gun in his face. "Look it here," Montana said pointing with the gun barrel. "Meet the end of yourself."

A soft, plosive putt-putt sound came out of my lower half.

"What," Montana said, "the fuck was that?"

"Buzz's rearend is fumy," said Hoot. Earl Suggs, on his back on the floor staring up at the gun, chortled.

"Yer sayin he broke wind," Montana said. "Speak straight, Hoot. Yer a fuckin shitpoke." Buzz put the barrel of his revolver against Suggs' teeth.

"The expulsion of vapor is an ordinary if odorous function. And you, Montana, don't amount to the shitgas of an overgrown cootie."

"Hey now," I said, "I toot when I got the jitters." I left the cover of the magazine rack behind. "Ain't nobody killing nobody," I said.

"Exceptin me," said Montana.

"I'll gun you down, Montana," I said, "I'm too scared not to." Holding my six-gun two-handed, my palms felt carved of soap stone.

The entire Texaco gently shivered and trembled.

"Montana White," Hoot said.

"Go on," said Montana. Earl Suggs' teeth scraped against Montana's gun steel. Lastlight glittered from every reflective surface.

"You are an unfortunate example of our species."

"Huh?"

"I say I've a wart that's brainier than you."

"Can I see it?" Montana's curious face was a study in divine permutation. The floor gently rose and fell back. The wood of the walls gave a low groan.

Montana withdrew the gun from Earl Suggs' face, took a step back, and began fumbling through his own pockets.

"I am near to fulminating," Hoot said. "Suggs, you're a sorry excuse for a victim."

"Well, you ain't much of a robber."

"Listen," I said, "anyone else notice the world's not as solid as it's supposed to be?" I felt a little bit frantic but tried not to show.

"In the future," Hoot said, "we case the clerks for intellectual potential. This has been like conversing with a potato."

A hill rolled across the floor. The earth rumbled.

"Christ," I said, "wake up!"

Montana White pulled a stick of dynamite from a pocket. "Suggs," Montana said, "Yer gonna die." He plucked a pack of matches from the countertop.

"Set the explosives down," said Hoot. "Me and you, Montana, have come to an end."

"Come on now," I said. Out the window, the sky was dark plum-colored. I heard the valves of my heart. The earth skipped and stuttered.

"Hosspiss," Montana said, "let's kick Earl's bucket." Montana said he meant to kill hundreds before he led the law into a box canyon. Tonight we'd lay up. He sparked a match; lit the fuse. The cock of one shoulder told us he didn't much give a damn.

"Sweet Mercy," I squealed, "I ain't set to die."

The light glared. The chrome shone. The fuse burned.

Hoot Rawley grabbed Montana by the arm and slung him toward the doors. He put a boot to Montana's chest and kicked him outside. "You," Hoot said, "I'm gonna have to kill." This was the plainest language I'd ever heard from him. Beneath the Texaco sign, Montana stumbled and straightened. He whipped his arm backward and then forward and tossed the dynamite high and far toward the pair of Japanese maples. My dog, Royal, sprinted after.

Montana went for his six-gun but Hoot backhanded it aside. Hoot hoisted Montana off the ground by belt and throat and tossed him like a loaf of bread. Montana landed hard; wrenched his shoulder; chipped a tooth.

Montana White stood, shook himself like a wet dog, squared his shoulders.

Hoot slunk toward Montana like calamity afoot.

"Hoot," I called, "shouldn't we split?" I may have been a bit teary-eyed.

"Sure thing," Hoot said, "but I've a loose end to attend to." Like a mirage, Hoot said, the future lay to the south of us, in the desert. Youth lay behind us. We'd find us an alcove and lay up. Most of us were headed to where outlaws belonged. The desert. Cacti. Saguaro and prickly pear. Dunes carved in sand.

The earth heaved. Underneath the Japanese maples, Royal pushed the dynamite with his nose. Red leaves fluttered around him. My heart seized. "Royal," I yelled, "Royal!"

Hoot spoke on. Our Illinois prairies turned suburbs offered nothing, he said; we were after the heat of the desert. We were wizened now, Hoot said, couldn't we all see it? We'd sling our bags; buckle our gear; cinch our leathers; and head out. Yeah, we'd aged good. We'd come out the far side of youth pretty much okay. "We're out to loose ourselves upon the world," Hoot said, "only Montana ain't going with us."

"You dirty browneye," Montana said.

"Montana," Hoot said, "prepare yourself to expire."

The earth split. Or maybe it didn't split, but the quaking made us feel like it meant to. The air whiplashed, and the cement beneath our feet rolled in waves. I pitched and stumbled. The chestnut trees tilted to unhealthy angles. Swallows rose in numbers that darkened the sky. The air was atwitter.

Under the Japanese maples, Royal jawed the stick of dynamite. He cast his eyes toward the mass of birds. On all fours, I clutched at the shimmying ground. "No, Royal!" I called, "No!"

Gasoline geysered out of ruptured pipes, fountained into the air, and sprinkled down on us. For a second, the rain felt pretty nice, heady and delirious, before it stung the eyes fierce, and stunk to high heaven. The earth quit grumbling. I stood stunned with my palms upturned watching the last light prism through falling gas, but Hoot and Montana barely took notice. They advanced continentally. They were going to collide. There was gravity involved.

Royal lay on the ground, dynamite between forepaws, chewing on the stick like a bone. The fuse glowed.

Hoot was saying something about each of us mocking the other with the sight of what we might have known.

Earl Suggs opened the door to the Texaco; said, "You boys better come on in out of that gasoline." He fanned himself with his baseball cap and breathed fumes.

Then, over by the Japanese maples, the dynamite exploded. Royal held the stick in his mouth and then came flame and bluc smoke and a concussion we felt carried on the air like a gust of gale-force wind. The red maple leaves lifted skyward. Bloodgouts and furstrips and flesh hung among branches. Then the wet sound of body parts falling.

"Shit," Earl Suggs mouthed at me, "that your mutt?"

I hunkered in the doorway to the Texaco, out of the gas rain, and cried silently. Earl came out under the eave, plucked me up, and held me. Hoot and Montana paid no mind. They faced each other and traveled in opposite directions on a single line. One of them would have to get trampled.

I pointed toward the blackened Japanese maples and what once had been my dog.

To the north lay the town, and to the south what we thought might be the dark heart of the country. Earl Suggs guided me, red-faced and tear-stained, to a lawn chair sitting under the eave. The moon reared up full. About half the chestnut trees had laid themselves down. Bats and swallows flittered above us. Gas fell in sheets from the roof. We couldn't hear much but a solid hum.

The maple trees dripped dog. We were quiet, or, if we weren't, we couldn't hear ourselves. The stillness of the air, the suspension of dust, the solidity of last light. A far-off cow lowed. I stared at the fire around the base of the elms.

Night was a half-lowered veil.

The peril and sorrow of the moment—the fall of gasoline, the nearby fire, the rain of dog—was as fetching as desire itself, and we figured right then, as certain as we knew six-guns and neckerchiefs accompanied out-lawry, that Hoot Rawley was dead on: talk was what we'd loosed upon the world and—even as Montana and Hoot collided in a shower of sparks, and the last rays of sun jumped over the edge of our earth, and I, the crybaby, leaned back in the lawn chair and fell over—we saw all our words, freed of tone and inflection, bending their way through the prairie grass and rising up like swallows, higher and higher. And never falling back.

The Language of Men Who Speak of What They Do Not Understand

WE BEGIN WITH the low hum of cicadas. The reflection of fire in the windows. The alternating rattle and clack of wind-blown tree limbs. Night moans that Holiday Clearwater says come from the ground. But Holiday is four; we forgive her. She often ties her shoes together and hops from point A to point B in imitation of a rabbit. Currently, she has a crow feather tied in her hair. Cirrus clouds striate the late afternoon sky with geometrical precision. In the east, the moon looks like a rumor of itself. Fluttering aspens shiver in the cool wind with less vigor than Owen Tatum Clearwater's right hand as it moves to his sister's shoulder. June Clearwater.

"Conceivably she's right, O," June says. She calls him O.

"Groaning's from trees," says Owen, "in the wind."

"I know."

"…"

"Two thousand," June says glancing at Holiday, "*d-e-a-d* this year in a catalog of bombings."

"Oh."

"Fifeteen *r-a-p-e-d* in the Tri-county area."

"Christ, Juney, *shhhhh.*"

"Three decapitations."

"Daddy, what's de-cap-stations?" says Holiday.

"Like popping the top of a canned soda," Owen says. "June, I don't follow."

"Everything's gone haywire," June says. "Dad laid up as he is."

"Laid up? This isn't passing, Juney."

"It's a figure of speech."

Owen, June, and Holiday sit at a booth on the side porch of the Rock Bar & Grill. A four-wheel drive kicks up dust as it wheels through the unpaved parking lot. We hear the sharp cracking of pine logs from the indoor fireplace. Holiday draws stick figures in crayon on her paper menu. She draws a thick-lined figure with the rear of the crayon and says how this stick figure's a real fatty among stick figures.

"I'm not doing well, O," June says.

"Juney, you're doing real well."

"No. Mnemonic skills are going. I can't remember anything."

"You're doing *real well.*"

"Waking up frightened," June says, "how I may have left the stove on."

"Happens."

"Going back outside twice in a row to ensure I locked the car door, turned the lights off."

"I guess my blood pressure's a tad high," says Owen.

"How high?"

"160 over 105."

"Not bad. What's happening with your hair?"

"Going A.W.O.L."

"I'm weeping over daytime TV," says June.

"I woke up around oneish last night," Owen says, "with Holly on the couch not even twitching. Still as midnight. I was sure she'd *d-i-e-d.*"

"Anymore when I gaze at the clouds," June says, "they only take the shape of common barnyard animals."

"I'm *wishing* Dad could call me a fuckhead," says Owen.

"I had this episodic dream," June says, "where Dad said how it would be good to get off this jerkwater world."

"A lift-off without gusto."

"I've become more headache than human," says June.

"Holly won't sleep with her night light on," Owen says, "she doesn't want the monsters to see her."

"Smart kid."

Hayward, Hayward thinks, *Hayward Clearwater, that's me.* He sees an off-white man in a white coat in front of a white wall that flickers between now and then. The pearly surface dances with images from Super 8 flicks that Hayward used to show-off to his kids, O and Juney. But his wall never smelled like this, like alcohol and lemon. Had he been drinking? *Where the hell's O*, Hayward thinks, *shouldn't he always be here?* The whitecoat has an impossibly large mouth that moves in slow-mo as he waves his hands in a crisscross fashion. The man's mouth says the name Dr. Ernesto R. Espiritu; mentions how he, Hayward B. Clearwater, is in the capable hands of Morphine and Dilaudid, which Hayward classifies as the names of either Greek or Roman gods. Hayward's field of vision consists of the wall, a TV mounted near the ceiling, and, far to the left, a window through which he can see nothing but blue. The man, and Hayward delves his brain to recall the name Espiritu, rattles on about how Hayward's in the I.C.U. at the Doctors' Hospital of Beloit. *Hemorrhage*, Espiritu says, *seat of consciousness, pons, brains stem, medulla oblongata, parasympathetic.* Hayward has half a mind to wrap his hands around this pipsqueak's wispy throat and squeeze the truth from him. Where's O and Juney? If anything's wrong with them he'll hold this bastard personally responsible. He's gonna remove this unnamed whitecoat's spine! No, not unnamed but titled Esperanza, no,

Saspirilla, yes, no, *Espiritu!* Hayward's body doesn't respond as he wills his muscles to leap from the bed and wreak havoc, though he's fairly certain he feels a twitching in his calves. He can, he realizes, with effort move his eyes. The whitecoat starts. Good, Espiritu says, please wiggle your left toes. Hayward's vision seems to zoom in and out again. If he ever gets out of this, Hayward thinks, his first act will be the brutal murder of this bastard Espiritu. Hayward attempts to wiggle his left toes. Did they move? Good, says the whitecoat while the corners of his mouth move down.

Indistinguishable foreign names are announced over the intercom. Someone outside his room chortles, someone moos. A series of blinding flashes is followed by laughter and the whirring sound of a projector. Hayward realizes that while he breathes, he can't control his breathing. A large tubular device is lodged in his throat. Someone touches his thigh. A nurse who wears the face of his dead wife rolls him on his side and works his legs back and forth. The woman is his wife, Candace. Candace wears a placard pinned before her left breast that reads LISA NOON, R.N. She says something regarding catheterization that Hayward represses. The R.N. channels the voice of Hayward's dead wife. Candace, he tries to say, please scratch the small of my back; Caddy could you find O and Juney, could you tell me what's happened, could you fetch a glass of orange juice, or rub my feet, or turn the radio off this country station and on to NPR, or tell me if memory can slip out the back of one's head, or apply some Vaseline to my lips, or just sit down beside me and tell me again how we fell in love. Caddy? Caddy? Son of sweet whores he couldn't open his eyes, did he have a body any longer? Maybe now he was a thingamajig, a cog, a loose wheel, soundless and dumb. Her fingers walk up his back, her lips press hot against his ear, breath wind-sweeps his gray matter as she whispers didn't he remember how they'd met during swim lessons at the YMCA where greedy-eyed he had watched her dive between lines of Styrofoam buoys until she climbed out of the water and he casually mentioned how she dove about as well as a donkey. She called him a pissant, a throwback, and a bore, but her thoughts, she later told Hayward, had been in a different key, focusing on his muscular calves, his single dimple, his shoulders that looked thick enough to bear the weight of ages. He asked her out for tea, for pizza and beer, for coffee, for cookies and a nightcap, until over eggs and milk in the morning she'd said she wanted someone fascinated by the physics of laughter, someone who wore suspenders, who liked to doublestraw a Slurpee, someone whose faith had wrinkled like fruit but not disappeared entirely, who had a certain Thoreau-style self-reliance, who wasn't bowlegged, someone who would follow her out of blind love and sighted trust as deep as the reaches of space, who listened to Miles Davis and Coltrane up close to the tweeter, who was a sexual athlete and made of a stern stuffing (infused with poetic fury but free of the vainglorious), someone who made the same unreasonable demands in return, and who said gesundheit, and for whom she defined the empyrean, not to mention all experience, Gestalt get bent. *Shit*, Hayward said, he was her man with just one question, what did empyrean mean? Candace said Hayward would never be able to define a term like *viridescence,* and had a vocabulary composed entirely of curse words. Grab my hand you two-bit floozy, Hayward said, don't let go no matter what I call you.

WE HEAR GEESE cry overhead. The sun perches low on the horizon. At the Rock Bar & Grill, June stares at the reflection of fire in the window. Holiday naps curled against Owen. A crow calls and Owen straightens the feather in Holiday's hair. We see a line of oncoming headlights on the just-visible highway, the organic light from oil lamps illuminating the porch, and how the almost-perceptible lengthening of shadows echoes the movement of time. We hear the clatter of flatware, an infant's warbling wail, the desperate cries for the overburdened waitress, the symphonic call of a thousand crickets, the dull electrical drone of an unseen transformer. Shadows lengthen to converge into evening.

"What'll we do, Juney?"

"Squat on our haunches. Wait. Hope, I guess. Stick together."

"I don't believe in the future anymore."

"No?"

The whoosh and flap of unseen wings, the elephantine roll of incoming clouds, the hurrays and hurrahs from indoors, a train's whistle, the humps of distant hills like breasts, yellowed grass in dim light looking like white hair, cloud masses breaking to reveal bits of bruised sky, the moon interrupted.

"I'm old," says Owen.

"You're not old."

"Well, I'm older."

"I guess we all are."

"So we do nothing." Owen stares into his coffee; he fondles the napkin dispenser, revolving it clockwise in his hands. He squeezes. "Holly's going to have no grandparents," he says. At her name, Holiday opens her mouth wide, feels her loose front tooth with an index finger, and sits up.

"You visiting Dad tonight?" June says.

"Uh huh."

"Give him my love." Willows turn raven-haired with dusk, the radio murmurs in pianissimo, someone inside speaks in pidgin English. The slam of a pick-up's hood, the buzz of errant yellow-jackets, the flicker and flash of moon-blanched leaves akin to tumbling water, the tickle of a cold breeze on the warm night, the curved line of haloed street lamps bordering the highway, the tonguelike movements of pussy willows under wind, the undulant hoot of unknown birds. Insect and small mammal calls like a catalog of glory or a hymnal paying homage to here-and-now, nitty-gritty *is*ness. A Siamese chewing its forepaws, the crinkle of newspaper, white holiday lights decking the gutters like substitute stars.

"When's Grandpa gunna read me *Goodnight Moon*?" Holiday says.

"We're not sure, Holly," says June.

"Soon?"

"*I'll* read to you."

The sky starts spitting water and ice. Birch trees creak under the wind's pressure; a chorus of hounds begin to howl and keen. Hail against the roof sounds like muffled drums. The night quails, the clouds groan. We know how moans have mouths.

Espiritu waves a foreign M.D. into Hayward's room, points excitedly at his charts, and speaks multi-syllabic nonsense. *Semi-vegetative*, Espiritu says, *extensive hemorrhagic damage to the cerebellum, 1000 to 1 against.* To Hayward it sounds as though Espiritu's brand of scientific explanation resorts to strange divinities. A whitecoat who calls herself an R.N. wipes Hayward's forehead with a damp hand towel, and he can't tell for sure but he thinks she's softly crying. *O*, Hayward thinks, *is that you O? Why are there three of you?* June is in the room, sitting cross legged on a chair beside the bed and twisting her long hair between her fingers, but Hayward blinks and the chair is empty. He hears the sound of ice on glass; some loudmouth explains how in the I.C.U. it's best to steer clear of words containing a D, or an E, or an A, or a T, or an H even. *Something's gone terribly wrong with my eyes, O. Owen, can you hear my thoughts? I think my body's fallen asleep for good, my boy.* Candace's there flickering flirtatiously like a candle in the corner, whispering a variation of the AA motto: hand jobs grant me the serenity to accept things I cannot change, etcetera etcetera. *Medically speaking, a poltergeist has been set loose in my mind.* Someone, either June or Owen, holds a series of Polaroids in front of Hayward but he makes out nothing but blotches of color. *I'm guessing I ain't too pretty, more or less reduced to eyesore. I've spoken more evil per square word than most; told woebegone lies to defrock a girl's breasts; laughed watching a street boxer vomit his teeth. Still not sure what I've done was bad.* A voice claims one blotch of purple is Hayward's granddaughter Holiday, a smudge of red represents his brick home, a dash of yellow his spirit. Hayward feels colder than he's ever felt. He's pretty sure the M.D., who glances at his charts and uses the name of the god Dilaudid in vain, couldn't be older than age eight. O's mouth is a fat O. *Son. . . Son! If only I could squeeze your hand, O. I'm not leaving you, boy, not by choice. I can't die, I've only made it through the T's in my En- cyclopedia Britannica, there's still candy bars I've never eaten, like the Zagnut. I've yet to show you and June how to make yourself look absent of fear through facial calisthenics, quick-talking, feints toward the eternal.* The R.N. rotates I.V. solutions overhead. Owen, sitting on the edge of the bed holding Hay- ward's hand, asks Hayward to wiggle his left toes as a way to say he loves him. A disembodied voice from outside his room laughs and tells someone else how fishing's always been in his blood like an antibody against the quote mechanization of civilization unquote. Hayward's left toes wiggle. *Mainly I believed mine was a story about luck, what came to me fell out of no- where, of flipped coins telling me lambskin not latex, of you O, and Juney, and Caddy, showing me how people were more than social security numbers, and where brawn and vigor came from, and how some times and some people strad- dle the human and the holy like bridges.* Hayward remembers how he filmed Candace and June fishing the Kishwaukee at a location so remote Candace took her top off and flaunted her pregnancy and pink nipples. *You never be- lieved me when I told you, O, but this is one of those events bigger than me.* June, age four, slipped in the milky Kishwaukee over and over again, but Never, the chocolate lab generally called Neve, fished her out with a gentle jaw, while, behind the Super 8, Hayward worried about life-yet-to-come, about omens, about how the obstetrician's forceps had left a minuscule divot by June's hairline that spoke to Hayward of miscarriages, compound fractures, chicken pox, and love gone awry. *I'm not ready. I'm afraid.* Candace had dismissed Hayward's fear with a term he didn't understand: senescence. Candace'd just started to show with the as-yet-unnamed Owen, and she had turned back to the OB/GYN talk, the qualities of 2nd borns, a list of names like Joseph for god, or Adam for numbers among men, or Victor for sport, or William for the Swiss and conquering love, or Thomas for flight and electrical fires, and John for graciousness and wine made of corn, or Henry for Henry VIII and lost minds, or Richard for kings and the sublime. *The ceiling's raising on me like a flue channeling toward a less-than-half believed in hereafter.* Candace smiled. *The nights suffocate like gasoline rags.* Hayward filmed June, blow-up yellow flotations wrapped around her arms, hanging to Never as she paddled in circles. *The white wall speaks the color of surrender.* Maybe Owen, Hayward said, for your Grandpa and the celebration of past times.

WE SEE HOW the pink neon sign, which reads Rock Bar & Grill, blinks in two second intervals. Holiday tugs at a waitress's apron and says how she'll need two or three cherry pies.

"It's been three weeks, right?" says Owen.

"Twenty-four days," June says.

"What gets me is how I don't know if that's a good sign or bad."

"…"

Holiday empties sugar packets on to the table, making what she describes as a mole hill. Under her breath, Holiday hums. June folds napkins into complex and unidentifiable shapes.

"I can breathe through my ears," Holiday says.

"Remarkable!" says June.

"Huh?" says Holiday.

HAYWARD, CADDY, JUNEY, and O, age nine, lollygag in the unused field adjacent to the All Saints cemetery. Caddy, red scarved and hatted, calls the type of day Decembral. Never, tinged with white on the edges of her nose, sprints to Juney and to O like a clockwork go-between. Bells play at St. Peter's and, as Hayward remembers it, Caddy says the word *tintinnabulation.* Hayward doesn't know the meaning, and figures, as Caddy knows, his ignorance doesn't matter much. O and Never wrestle until O manages to put the dog in a full nelson. Juney relates to Caddy how she thinks O ought to let that poor dog go. Hayward, squatting on his haunches, tells O how Caddy and him are really concerned about this running away business, twice in the last six months, and how it scares him, Hayward, senseless. O's running away sets his heart pounding, Hayward says, gives him the sweats, makes his nose run and his lungs work overtime. They stand beneath the winter-bare arms of an oak tree. O, voice an instrument of nosework, says how he'd got the swiftest time climbing the monkey rope in gym, how his favorite ever meal is fish-and-chips, how he'd just learned the word *pre-ternatural* for a vocab test and it fit him to a T, how K.C. Norse had called him a fraidy-cat for no reason and he, O, had been forced to bend K.C. into a pretzel, how this pretzel-bending had earned him a nickname, The Colossus. O says he runs because he's got to keep on the move, confound notions of the expected, but he didn't know he'd scared Hayward. He's real, real sorry, honest to God. Never chews on O's pant leg. Hayward and Caddy huddle together against the oak tree. According to O, the entire Norse clan are enemies of the red-blooded. Caddy put her hands in Hayward's front jeans pocket, whispering in his ear of bedroom pleasures involving the viscera. Just beyond the branches of the oak tree, Juney dizzies herself by twirling in circles. Hayward, scratching his back against the oak's bark, asks The Colossus what he thinks of his new nickname, and O says it's hunky dorey. A light, filmy snow begins to fall.

Someone, the R.N. who has tits like halved cantaloupes Hayward thinks, holds a squarish piece of stiff paper about three inches from his eyes. Hayward feels convinced they have surreptitiously replaced his mattress with a block of steel. He strains to keep his eyes open. When closed, he sees letters swim on the inside of his eyelids. Hayward thinks he can make out the inky black and chalky white of newsprint. Behind his eyelids, letters resolve into legible order.

    Hayward B. Clearwater

    Hayward B. Clearwater, 61, died at 12:59 a.m. Thursday, May 25, 1993 in the Doctors Hospital of Beloit. Survivors include son, Owen Clearwater of Beloit; daughter, June Clearwater of Springfield; and grand-daughter, Holiday

Clearwater of Beloit. Predeceased by beloved wife, Candace Clearwater.

Services at 10:30 a.m. Monday, May 29, in Julian-Poorman-Welte Funeral Home, with Rev. Archibald B. Christianson officiating. Burial in Scandinavian Cemetery. Memorials in care of the family.

The R.N., by the soft moist feel of it, sponge-bathes Hayward. He feels that it is possible, even probable, she is using her tongue. Suddenly, Hayward suspects, by the blurred and distorted quality of his vision, that either his entire body or just his head has been placed underwater. He hears a slight scratching sound and an eerie high-pitched lowing that he feels must be the mourning TINTINNAB-ULATION of whales.

Never, rooting in a pile of loose dirt, unearths a skull. Bones between her teeth, she trots it to Hayward. Hayward mentions how the skull has horns, how the jaw bone runs the length of his forearm, how the eye sockets could fit a tennis ball. Caddy refers to the skull as remains. Cow, Hayward says. Juney fingers the holes in the rear of the skull and says how the brain used to be somewhere in there. The skull, O says, may be cow but the teeth sure look human to him. Never sits next to the dirt pile gnawing on a loose vertebrae. Caddy says the whole scene gives her the heebie-jeebies; nudging Hayward in the thigh, she asks if he can't think of anything better they could do, at home.

O asks Hayward how the cow died; Hayward says death is one of those items bigger than him.

There is the hollow sound of plastic wheels on tile. Hayward sees the mince-minded nail-biter with the brainworks of a lima bean, that gallivant Espiritu, pop his head in. Out the single window, the moon looks feeble and semi-translucent like a fingernail clipping.

Caddy, with thin paper and charcoal, has made a grave rubbing that reads, **For he makes a good end who dies loving well**. Hayward takes

Owen by the shoulder and says so please, for his sake, don't go running off anymore O. Sometimes, Caddy says, she thinks of life and death as but two scenes in a heart-felt phantasmagoria.

"Oh no," Holiday says, "I've lost it!"

"What, honey?"

"I forgot."

"We're leaving, Holly."

"Can I get another sundae? With strawberries."

"No."

"Just a cookie?"

"Let's go."

"A quarter for candy?"

"…"

We see night has blanketed the landscape. Owen tells Holiday to give June a kiss good-bye. June covers her face with cupped hands; Owen looks away.

"I'm not tired," Holiday says.

"No?" June says, "I'm quite tired."

"I'm not going to bed."

"Really? What'll you do then?"

Holiday shrugs her shoulders, lifts her chin high as she thinks a minute, and suggests they stay up late telling ghost stories and eating marshmallows. Owen lifts Holiday to his shoulders. Holiday says that from way up here she can see how everything's okay.

"Daddy, you okay?"

"Sure, Holly, Daddy's fine."

Caddy uses a cool white washcloth to wipe Hayward's face; she rubs his neck with her thumbs just the way she always used to. Hayward considers the implausibility of the no-man of big-league ken.

Grab hold of your heart, Hayward thinks he hears the R.N. say.

Juney, slack-jawed and pale-skinned, squats next to the bed dressing her plastic horse in a red outfit. O is absent, Hayward notes, probably run away again. The respirator continues to inflate and deflate lungs. *Caddy*, Hayward thinks, *please fetch O*. For a split second the whole Clearwater family sits on the leather couch watching the television play *A Miracle on 34th Street*. Espiritu seems to have been captured by time-lapse photography as he waves a kidney-shaped pan and gesticulates with his fingers and before Hayward's own eyes begins a rapid SENESCENCE, begins to lose his youthful looks: his spine bows, his flesh wilts, his face thins, wrinkles, and grays. Juney's beside the bed squeezing Hayward's hand. It occurs to Hayward how the blue-jumpsuited cleaning man who haunts his room at night before looking Hayward dead in the eyes and saying, *You sure sick mutherfucker,* is the only person not treating him with kid gloves, and how he could no longer tell the difference between quote real life unquote and hallucinations, and how silly of him to think There But By The Grace and so on, and how the moonlight coming in the window made his tiny landscape look desolate and ghost-like and the visiting R.N.s like specters of their former selves, and how, in one of those Polaroids, O and Juney sit on his leather couch with sweet Holly on the floor and all three glance furtively toward the recliner where Hayward ought to be but isn't, and, facing facts, sex is pretty much out of the question ever again, and how finally he felt shit-sure of something if only how the sum of his physiological parts couldn't define Hayward B. Clearwater as whole. But if you included O and Juney and Holiday as parts of him, then maybe he'd allow how you could. With every useless cell he ached to drink a short glass of Johnnie Walker Black, to teach Holly how to count one-mississippi, two-mississippi, three-mississippi. Or to explain how some old-timey notions of give-and-take led him to understand finally at the ripe age of fifty-three, approximately forty-one years too late, how in playing shoot-'em-up one couldn't always play the cowboy or the Indian. (*O! where are you O?*) The blue jumpsuit empties a waste-paper basket and crosses himself out of respect for the dead. *Who's dead?* Hayward thinks. The lights flicker rapidly, revealing the room in surreal flashes that remind Hayward of the lapse of years. The world is made of papier-mâché.

O arrives as the antithesis of Espiritu, in a slow *VIRIDESCENCE* where his bodily composition moves against time. Facial features recapture a former innocence. Smile lines unfold. Hairline proceeds. Taking a seat in the bedside chair, his legs shorten so they dangle above the ground. O wiggles his toes furiously. Hayward's eyes focus on Owen.

Please don't run away again, O! I thought you'd run off to fight the Norse. I thought you'd been caught. By kidnappers, or worse. Joined some revolutionary movement. I thought you'd been found been tortured been killed. I thought you'd left me, I don't know, I just, I thought… I'm glad you're home.

Someone in the room weeps like their heart's breaking.

"Daddy, I got things to tell."

"Things? How many?"

"Three hundurd things."

"Good or bad?"

"Mosty bad."

"Bad huh?"

"I'm not ascared."

"No?"

"Not even one little."

"Well, good."

"Are you ascared?"

"Just a bit."

"Shouldna be."

"No?"

"I got thoughts can split stuff in two."

Wretchedness

I.

Salvation went like this: I bulleted snowballs single-handed—the right was occupied with a tumbler of gin—at two youngsters, whose forgotten names caused me to question the nature of memory, on a snow-covered lawn that wasn't mine when Carmen, my on-again off-again spouse, brought her father, Boyd E. Plumley Jr., and her sister's second husband, Deputy Cooke, screeching to a halt on the two-lane in the Deputy's cruiser, flashing emergency colors. The sky swam in shades of red wine. The three slamming doors concussed simultaneously. My gin tasted like high spirits. Carmen (of off-the-scale skin-deep beauty), Boyd E. Plumley Jr. (of the hairy double-barreled chest), and Deputy Cooke (of the open fly) walked to the edge of the lawn, and I, manifold in my blameworthiness, hollered: "One more single misstep, Deputy Cooke, I'll whip your puny behind!"

"Elias Matterhorn," Deputy Cooke said, "you're willy-nilly with rum." The Deputy chewed his words slowly.

"Not just yet," I said.

Deputy Cooke doffed his hat and raked his fingers through his hair. My swigged gin upended the earth and lay me flat in the snow. Gray blanketed the sky. Ice hugged tree limbs. The children, one boy and one girl, sat down on my right and began tossing handfuls of powder over my head. Closing my eyes, I was overcome by the feeling that, like a snow angel, I was little more than an impression left behind.

"Kids," I said, "just to key you in, the bulk of my years were spent as a seventh grade teacher. You can trust me—what're your names?"

"Daisy Hoklin," said the girl, "and my brother, Noel." Daisy's features lay buried under the hood of her pink snowsuit; Noel stood as tall as a belly button.

"This your house?" I gestured behind my head with a thumb. Under two feet of snow, the roof resembled a ski slope. Red and green lights ran with the gutters.

"Sure is," said Daisy.

"You're drunk, mister," Noel said. His mittens caused his hands to resemble flippers.

"What're you up to here, Elias?" called the Deputy. He stood on the sidewalk, twenty-five feet away. His breath billowed into a cloud as solid as a cartoonist's dialogue balloon.

"I'm in the midst of learning the tango," I said. "I've got some skill with the castanets. I've mastered subtlety, not to mention penmanship. I'm building a canoe with long smooth lines that puts one in mind of what women ought to be."

"Now Elias," said Deputy Cooke, "you're talking foolishness. This here ain't your lawn. You got to move."

"Be with you in a jiffy," I called. "Say, Carmen?"

"I'm here, honey."

"What's with the reinforcements?"

"Listen," said Carmen. She paused to draw a breath. "Your cousin Jacob died."

My mind recalled the face of Granddaddy Matterhorn—the spitting image of cousin Jacob—who'd been taken by tornado. "Little tow-headed Jacob Matterhorn?"

"Well, he'd lost most of that hair, but that's right."

A gust of wind bullwhipped a sapling. Snowflakes blew horizontally. In the face of the tornado, Granddaddy Matterhorn had carried Jacob and me to the cellar, returned upstairs for his dachshund, and been carried away.

"Jacob *C.* Matterhorn," I asked Carmen, "for whom I played best man?'

"You only know the one, Elias."

"What in goddamn hell he ever do? *You answer me that!*"

Feeling my frozen head, I found it wrapped with my only handkerchief (printed with lion cubs), and noted that my recent past was a breed of memory as indiscernible as the future. I was thinking of propensities for dimness, about the labyrinthian, about my interior—slick as hot tar, dark as a black hole. I recalled how Uncle Timothy, Jacob's father, came to nothing but a story about an over-sized, big-eared man who gave his life to Vietnam. How my nephew, Lucas, had lost his bearing in the Alleghenies, ran in the direction of freedom, and been caught by blizzards or buzzards or cold. How Aunt Annie got struck by lightning and died kicking. How someone I'd mostly forgotten, either Franny or Beth, sleep-walked into the river and drowned. How they died, my family, fast as fruit flies and most often weren't missed.

Noel tossed a snowball at Daisy. My tumbler didn't hold enough gin. The cold pinched my chest. Carmen waved me toward her with broad arm gestures.

"Elias," Carmen said. "What're you gunna do?"

"Sit with these kids. Drink till the snow dissolves." I gestured to either side with my hands. Boyd E. Plumley Jr. rested his wrists across his round belly; Deputy Cooke cocked his arms at his sides like a gunslinger.

"You don't belong to booze," Carmen said, "you're mine."

"True," I said. "My love's like a Chinese finger puzzle. Booze is fleeting, maybe inconsequential."

"Elias," said Deputy Cooke, "I'm gonna remove you from this lawn."

"Why don't you come in out of the snow?" asked Carmen.

"I showed Jacob how to fish for bluegill," I said, "and how to tie a fisherman's bend. Taught him how to throw a curve ball, and how to use the aurora borealis as an aphrodisiac, and how even women made of ice have a soft underbelly. I introduced him to Helen, whom *he married* for crying out loud."

Deputy Cooke hitched his pants and took a step forward.

"You were his friend," said Carmen.

"He die of misery or spite?"

"Choked," said Carmen. "Turkey bone."

Deputy Cooke trod across the snow toward me. He socked one gloved hand into the other. Daisy and Noel tossed a snowball toward the sky. Hooking over a telephone wire, the packed snow splintered and tumbled earthward.

"Daisy. Noel," I said, "how'd you like to see the Deputy and me have at it?" Shaking the snow from my hair, I stood up. Everyone got a cordial invitation to admire the impression I'd left behind.

Deputy Cooke stepped up and fumbled at my wrists.

"C'mon Deputy," I said, "let's wrestle!" I grabbed Deputy Cooke by the arms. By the milky quality of his eyes, I inferred that he was adrift in trepidation, in hesitance and avoidance. His tongue caught in a pattern of stuttering that sounds like distant gunfire. *This boy trafficked in fear*. I wiggled him hard enough to rattle his noodle.

"Wake the fuck up!" I said. I shook him until his head nodded back and forth, as my daddy liked to do to me. We were nose to nose, the deputy and me. His hair quivered. His lips were the color of eggplant.

I tried to tackle Deputy Cooke. The Deputy evaded my lurch, tripped me with a boot, and laid me gently on the ground. Sitting on my back, the Deputy's gloved hands fumbled to herd my wrists together. Aided by the snow's slickness, I shimmied from underneath the Deputy's legs, shoved him forward, and ground his face in the snow. I announced to Daisy and Noel, who'd backed up against the house, that the textbook for mild success could be distilled to three items. Which, for their benefit, I was mighty pleased to relay.

Lying my full weight across the Deputy's body, I scissored my legs around his waist and stuck my tongue in his ear.

"One," I shouted, "in that which goes unsaid lies our chief concern. And, incidentally, let your hair grow out a little. You look a bit prissy."

The deputy bucked like a bull and sent me careening. I tore around the snow like a rabbit. I came at the Deputy from behind, screaming as loud and high as a newborn.

"Two: misfortune and loss pile up like foothills and mountains. Learn to spell circumnavigate."

I reached into Deputy Cooke's pants and wrenched his jockey shorts. As the Deputy clotheslined me, I yanked him toward me by his nose. I confounded him with fancy footwork, snuck his gun from its holster and buried it in the snow.

"Three: don't think too much about the future. What's up there's spinning like a kaleidoscope."

I leaped, massaged the Deputy's chest with my feet, knocked him flat-out and horizontal. Placing my lips to his ear, I whispered about the weight of abstraction, about my fondness for Nat King Cole, about my head feeling like a pressure cooker. I spoke about yardrules designed to measure what we've lost. About my great aunt Patricia going blind drinking wood alcohol; then having her throat ripped out by her seeing-eye dog. About my step-brother Thurston and his baby twins, Melinda and Mariah, going up with the house fire. About Aunt Victoria disappearing without a trace. About Jacob being ten times the man that either the deputy or I could ever hope to be.

As the Deputy pounded my midriff and I chafed his ear with my teeth, I gave him a number of words—*dearth, wage, glee, salivation*—so that he might understand something of my sweep and scale. I mentioned *blithe* and *annihilation*.

Snow worked its way under the hems of my coat. Cold insinuated my gray matter. Carmen and her father, Boyd E. Plumley Jr. stood open-mouthed on the sidewalk. I lost the gist of what I meant to say, foundered in the multiplicity of my thoughts, and emptied my belly's contents on Deputy Cooke's shirttails.

I inserted my finger in Deputy Cooke's open fly and wiggled.

"*Sweet Jesus!*" bellowed the Deputy.

"Ain't nobody coming to help you!" I yelled.

"Elias," said Carmen, "climb off a him."

"I'm drunk with fury!" I screamed. My hands, balled into fists, raised into the air. My lungs imploded. My eyes leaked fire.

Boyd E. Plumley Jr.—as sneaky and inexorable as time—plowed through the snow, used his palm like a hammer, and gave me what-for.

II.

Two nights later I slunk into All Nite Liquors with a five spot. Snow, piled against the walls, caused the building to resemble a blanched hill. A bell jingled as I opened the door.

Fragments of time had been paper-punched from my memory.

The clerk, with long thinning hair and spectacles, was the image of my Daddy. Daddy who'd knocked out half a dozen of my milk teeth with a tire iron, beat Jacob with his fists, and then flew town. I informed the sniveling clerk that I didn't believe in drink, it was for weak-willed folk who trust in Yeti, for ingrates and those without goals, for those whose sieve-like minds don't hold water.

The clerk said that's good because he don't believe in money.

We traded in brands of disbelief. The clerk, I surmised by his inspection, suspected the fiver of being counterfeit.

Bottle in tow, I flung open the door, reached up to ring the bell with a fist, and trod down the icy walk. I headed south on Meridian Road. The street remained unplowed, the sidewalk unshoveled. The snow stood above knee level. To either side of the road, towering oaks, branches parabolic with snow, made the road feel like a tunnel. A sweat-suited man high-stepped along the path where he imagined the sidewalk to be.

Clouds touched down in the snowfield created by the long stretch of front lawns. I was remembering Talmon Rhyne, my grandfather on my mother's side, who had been caught in a snowstorm and found frozen like an ice sculpture. Choking, I thought, may be preferable to freezing. The air smelled of fermentation. Ice began to fall from the sky.

As the man in the sweatsuit and I passed one another, he shoved me into a snowdrift. I toppled in slow motion. The atmosphere above swirled in monotonous gray. The sweatsuit was colored maroon.

"Your wallet," he said, "fork it over."

Finding my footing, I braced myself with one arm, stood, brushed the snow from my corduroys. "Look," I said, "I've been outdoors far too long. My feet are numb. My ass is damp."

"Your fucking money!" he said. He jabbed my shoulder. Underneath the hood, I saw dense eyebrows, a long hooked nose, slightly askew blue eyes.

"Flat busted," I said. "By God, you look familiar." He lanced a fist toward my nose. "Paddy?" I said.

I found myself back-floating in the snow. The oak limbs that rose above me were covered in a fine skin of ice. Feeling had deserted the left side of my head. I stretched my arms out to either side, my hands clutching at snow, to stop the ground from trembling. My nose swelled; my right eye failed to focus.

"Remember me, Paddy?" I said. "J.F.K. Middle School. Seventh grade."

"Middle School?" he said.

"That's right."

"Mr. Matterhorn?" he said. "Astronomy?"

"Bingo."

"You gave me a D," he said.

"Look, how about we let the D go? You come over tomorrow for ham and creamed corn. We'll talk about planetary alignment. Red dwarfs and quasars. Come on over, we'll talk about black holes." I told Paddy I'd come to shit. How, in the end, the seventh graders had seen through me. They'd told the principal that I was hollow, informed their parents that I was little but drunken ballyhoo and overly frank, sexually speaking. How I'd French-kissed the red-haired student teacher, Ms. Caramel, in the coatroom, and finally, *the little bastards*, through a crayon and paper campaign, got me fired.

"Jesus," said Paddy.

"There ain't crap to take from me."

"Pass me that vodka."

"This," I pointed at the bottle, "this here is mine. Though we could share." I patted the snow beside me. "Sit," I said.

Paddy pinched the thighs of his pants between thumb and forefinger, pulled upwards, and sat. The hardened external layer of snow crunched. I told how my Uncle Frederick drank until cirrhosis got his liver. How Aunt Myrtle and Cancer slipped away together in the night. How Grandma Matterhorn, who raised me after Daddy split, gave up her mind before her ghost. She couldn't recognize me. She communed with philodendrons and flowered wallpaper. She passed on peacefully in her sleep.

Wiping blood from my eye, I relayed to Paddy that I didn't hold his being a thief against him, no way no how. I mentioned something about times being hard. I told how when we were nine, my favorite cousin Jacob and me, working together, scored two goals in the after-school soccer game and raced home in cleats and shin-guards to tell Jacob's mom just what brand of champions we were turning out to be. How we raced inside, leaving the screen door open. How I thought I smelled toast burning. How we trailed bits of dirt across the carpet until, halfway through the living room and near the leather couch, we stopped. How I could only see her back, feet dangling inches above green kitchen tile. How her feet arched, toes splayed and point-ed earthward. Her hair hanging to mid back. Framed by the doorway, backlit by the kitchen's fluorescence, she dangled. She revolved. Her rose-colored lipstick applied freshly. Her eyes wide open. Her name—Ellen. I couldn't feel my heart beating. The bubbled white paint of the ceiling eclipsed the kitchen.

Paddy told me his grandmother'd been evicted, gone to live in a shel-
ter. His mother peddled favors of love. For the moment, he was making a
home of the street. "Sorry about the eye," said Paddy, "and your nose."

"Sorry about the D," I said. The thick snowfall limited our vision to a
few feet. I suggested to Paddy that we might be inside a snow globe. "Let's
go," I said, "the basement's finished. Even got its own door."

As we walked, I told how Aunt Janis lost her head in an explosion of
blood, gristle, and gray matter to a shotgun blast aimed elsewhere.

Paddy shared how his infant brother had been born with no spine.

"Not bad," I said. My niece Minnie, beneath the wide city sky, got raped
by a van load of strangers. They stole her voice and left her an empty vessel.
My step-brother, Carter, papa to Minnie, hunted himself an entire van
load of city folk, leaving behind a river of blood as wide as the Mississippi.

Paddy relayed how his father was a preacher who hobbied in sodomy.

"*Jesus*," I said. The snow fell in torrents. "Ellen's son. My cousin, Jacob.
He choked to death today."

"Today?" asked Paddy. I nodded. "Shit, *man*," said Paddy, "sorry to hear it."

"Feels as though I've lost an appendage."

III.

Our home, Carmen's and mine, loomed. My extremities were numb. My
legs propelled me forward. My coat had taken a leave of absence.

I let Paddy into the basement, advised relative silence, entered the
garage and swiped a hand along the side of my dusty canoe. She was rest-
ing, flat-bottomed, near the table saw. The light from the bulb hanging
above me circled the garage. The cracked mirror by the door reflected my
familiar copper eyes and graying hair. The three-day beard was a measure
of lassitude. The skin in close proximity to my left eye was a mixture of red
and purple. The white obfuscated by blood.

Snatching a can of paint thinner from the workbench, I opened the
door to the kitchen.

Carmen, in boxers and a lilac night shirt, bent to ogle the contents of the refrigerator. She straightened, pointed toward the paint thinner. "What's that for?" she said.

"For Jacob," I said, "and my cousin, Baylee."

"You know," said Carmen, "you ought to tell me more about your family."

"How's the Deputy?" I said. I decided against telling how my Uncle Samuel had been jailed for stifling his crying daughter, eight months old, by gagging her with a crew sock.

"Nothing but sore pride. How're you?"

"Ungodly sore. A mite tired. Addled by spirits." I didn't tell how, in order to educate Jacob and me about Jesus, my Daddy, toxic with hooch, had driven a roofing nail through Jacob's palm.

"Your eye's bleeding," said Carmen. "What happened to your nose?" Cupping my face gently with both hands, I noted that my nose, once as finely curved as a snow drift, bent sharply at the bridge.

"Must've stumbled." I didn't tell how Cousin Jacob and I'd worshipped Cousin Baylee. Cousin Baylee whose image did not surface without bruises. Darkened cheekbone, blackened eye, gashed temple, broken rib, missing tooth.

"You're a drunk, Elias."

"I know it." Baylee who once came out of his foster parent's bungalow after sunset, index finger broken and gums bleeding, to throw his arms over Jacob's and my shoulders and brag he couldn't feel pain.

"I'm leaving you, Elias."

"You haven't left already?" We'd pounded on each other's chests, laughed, and staggered about the garage like three-legged dogs. We lounged on Baylee's pallet, sniffing lighter fluid, until Baylee shared how one upcoming night, in the not-too-distant future, he intended on entering the bungalow, turning the gas stove to BROIL, and waiting with wooden matches.

"I mean I'm cutting town."

"Hoped you'd stay." We'd inhaled lighter fluid until our minds were left someplace behind us, dizzy and numb, and Baylee claimed the world stood wide open before us. Couldn't we see it?

"Just fucking look at you!"

"What about me?" Then, in the seventh grade, Jacob and I got off the school bus to find only the blackened concrete foundation where Baylee's bungalow had stood. We'd applauded.

"*Look at you*, Elias."

"Is it bad?"

"You're a sight to behold."

I sequestered myself in the bathroom. Porcelain shimmered under vanity lights. The seasonal shower curtain was printed with snowmen. The air smelled of opium-scented air freshener. A single window looked to the front lawn. Dousing a wad of toilet paper with paint thinner, I placed it under my crooked nose. I opened the top of the toilet tank to remove the pint of gin I'd stashed the Sunday before.

I cracked the bathroom door open. "Carmen," I said, "I've got something to ask you."

"Go on."

"You mind letting the basement to a mugger named Paddy?"

"A *mugger* named Paddy?"

"He's a good sort."

"A *good sort*?"

With my foot, I inched the door shut. I was thinking of Daddy and of Cousin Jacob. How Daddy's heart had quit pumping in Woolworth's two days before Christmas. How I hadn't seen him since Carmen made the free-range turkey for Thanksgiving. How, on his fire escape, Jacob grew a plant called love-in-the-mist in a mop bucket. How Jacob's wife, Helen, who's outlasted him, might be staring out their apartment windows and facing the blizzard alone.

Blown-air heat gusting from the vent dried my eyes.

I squatted on the toilet, eyelids like five pound weights and pulse like a metronome. The water running in the toilet sounded like whispered voices. I peered out the window. What greeted me seemed as mysterious as the future and as fetching as religion.

I stumbled backwards. Splashed my face with water. Blotted the dampness from my eyes. I swigged gin. Inhaled paint thinner. Pressed my eyes with my thumbs. Blinked repeatedly. The thinner and gin plumbed the depths of my brain and opened gates to worlds other than mine, calling forth thingumajiggers and something-or-others from the snow. Human shapes rose like ghosts through the trapdoors of a stage. The entire host in ballroom clothes as gossamer as spider's webbing, as white as the Christian soul.

I wiped the fog of my breath from the window. Before me lay a swirl of ice and snow lit by a single streetlamp and dancing headlights, and marching beneath, led by Uncle Thurston's twins, Melinda and Mariah, a parade of all the dead people I'd known. Melinda and Mariah, wrapped in white bandages, held long icicles like batons. The snowflakes were the size of saucers. There was Uncle Frederick, *by God*, in pearly overalls and waltzing alone. A dozen of my past students in white jumpsuits doing cartwheels and somersaults. Up ahead I saw Uncle Timothy scouting the lay of the land. There was Aunt Janis, Annie. Lucas pointing out the path and hollering directions while leading blind Aunt Patricia by the hand. And my old Daddy, in a white bathrobe, looking as forlorn as a whipped puppy.

Stumbling backwards, I pinched myself hard and watered down my fear with gin. I noticed that the gathering of so-and-sos and such-and-suches failed to leave prints in the snow.

Here came my Granddaddy, Talmon Matterhorn, wrapped in white furs; Franny and Beth still sleep-walking. Aunt Victoria guided the party with hand signals. I saw Martin, Myrtle, Leroy, Uncle Samuel. Ms. Caramel in a white teddy. There was Uncle Thurston on ice skates. Jacob in a double-breasted suit, white as the winterland, towing Baylee, free of bruises, on a sled.

Opening the window above the toilet, I stuck my head into the cold.

"*Where in goddamn hell you all been?*" I bellowed. The wind twisted my words to howling. My lips began to freeze, my ears turned numb. The spirits failed to answer.

"Carmen," I shouted, "you out there?"

"*Jesus,* Elias!" said Carmen. Her voice slipped under the bathroom door. "I'm right here. In the kitchen. Drinking chamomile."

"Oh," I said.

"Who you yelling to?" said Carmen.

"I think it's dead folks."

"They talk back?"

"Not yet."

There was Jacob's mother Ellen in a wedding dress with a train that stretched farther than the eye could see. Uncle Carter, in longjohns, gave his daughter Minnie a piggyback ride. Grandma Matterhorn, prattling on soundlessly to Daddy, seemed to be listing the kingdom, phylum, class, order, family, genus, and species of the human organism. My cousin Jacob, arms stretching out to his sides, encompassed my entire field of vision. He straightened the lapel of his double-breasted suit. I slipped my head and shoulders through the window. Leaning toward him, I felt as though the window sill had cut me in two. "Jacob," I called, "Jacob, let me in on what's happened."

"Elias," Carmen said, "you better come out of that bathroom."

"Be out in a minute."

Nearly all of the procession had moved beyond the reach of the streetlamp. Daddy and Ms. Caramel danced the flamenco. Ice swirled around them. Jacob and Baylee began stomping their feet. My eyes swelled, my throat constricted. I waved goodbye to Jacob and Baylee, winked at Ms. Caramel, nodded to Daddy. There were a million things I ought to have said. Snow fell as thick as insulation; wind blew sideways; headlights flickered across ice. Behind Jacob in the sled, Baylee seemed to be overtaken by laughter. Baylee's mouth opened wide, his sides shook soundlessly. Jacob, the funnybones, must've said something good.

"*Godfuckingdamnit, Jacob!*"

Jacob halted, leaned towards me, wiped ice from his eyes, and shrugged.

The wind moaned; snow plummeted from tree branches; the streetlamp cut out; and the outdoors steeped in darkness.

I straightened, mopped my face with a swatch of toilet paper, spat in the sink. "Okay, boys," I murmured, "my love life's waiting on me." I tossed a white hand towel outside into the snow.

Carmen hammered on the door. "I'm looking through the keyhole, Elias," she said, "looks a lot like you're naked."

My eyes took in my skin's contours. "Shit if it ain't true," I said.

"Do I need to fetch the Deputy?"

"I'm dog-eared, worn thin. My skin's translucent. How about I put some clothes on, then we sit a spell." Pulling on my boxers and T-shirt, I opened the bathroom door. I studied Carmen. High cheek bones, soft potbelly, cinnamon skin, ripe lips, curves that couldn't be drawn. "I feel like I haven't seen you in ages," I said.

"Sit where?" Her arms crossed over her chest.

"The couch. Better yet, my canoe."

"Your *canoe?*"

"Let's sit in the canoe and talk."

"Talk about what?" She rubbed her palms against her arms.

"I can't keep missing him like this. I can't." The accumulation on the roof caused low groans in the rafters. Cold air slipped in through unseen crevasses. Snow suppressed sound.

"You mean Jacob?" She was reaching an arm out toward me.

"How I feel, it's like a vital organ's missing."

"You ought to."

"I'm missing you, too."

"I'm not dead yet, Elias." She was making come-hither gestures with her hands as though she wanted to squeeze me until my flyaway parts converged.

"You're not dead yet?"

"No. Neither are you."

Concurrence

On Lexington Avenue in New York City, Aary Swenson, a boy of seven years, slipped his hand loose of the black mitten his father held. For twenty-one seconds, John Swenson, the boy's father, continued to hurry down the busy sidewalk. He towed the empty mitten. The boy—eyes as brown as turned earth—had stopped beside the Chrysler building. Pedestrians swirled around him. He was looking up.

A light snow fell. Contrails cut the sky. For the first time, Aary Swenson, at seven years old, imagined that from another position, from the oval passenger window of an airplane in the sky, he might disappear between the press of buildings.

In Woodstock, Illinois, in her single-story home, Andie Hanover née Burbank found a note left by her mother on the cherry kitchen table. Andie Hanover had the flu. Her pale skin was flushed. Her brown hair stuck to her face with sweat. She could hear her heart in her ears. Wakened by a cold draft, she had gotten out of bed just before noon, shuffled out of the bedroom, past the twin Dürer prints in the hallway, into the kitchen where the note—written on peach-colored stationery and scented with meadowsweets—lay tucked beneath a vase of daisies.

Andie Hanover's feet scraped the tile of the kitchen floor. She shivered with cold. Sun glared though the window above the sink. Andie Hanover sniffled and wiped her nose with her sleeve. Her mother had cleaned. The kitchen table, left untidied after yesterday's supper, had been swept of crumbs. The china, which Andie had abandoned in a stack near the sink, shined behind the glass of the hutch. The kitchen floor had been mopped. On the counter the pepper mill lay on its side. The steel of the faucet glimmered. The glass patio door was agape.

Andie Hanover née Burbank slid the patio door closed. The Gerber daisies on the table had begun to wilt. She stepped to the kitchen table, picked up her mother's note. *My baby girl*, she read. *I've gone to die. Don't fret yourself, dear. I love you so. We've all done the best we can. Bury me beside your father. You'll feel better soon.*

At noon, in the Greek Orthodox cemetery in Woodstock, Illinois, Helena Burbank, a woman of eighty, stood before the grave of her husband. Elms stood in rows. Box hedges ran in parallel lines. Helena Burbank remembered the fear in the tremble of her husband's lips as he died, of cardiac arrest, nearly forty years ago. Sitting on her husband's headstone, Helena unbuttoned her ankle-length cashmere coat. One end of her red scarf flapped in the wind. Her footprints, in the thin crust of snow, could lead her back toward home. Ice cracked in a tree. Her hands shook. Every muscle in her ached. Lately, she had been too weary to tell people how weary she felt. Helena ran her fingers across her husband's engraved name. The dying roses beside his gravestone were those she left last week. The grass beneath the inch of snow had yellowed and wilted. Helena Burbank drew a kitchen knife from her coat pocket. She set the knife at the base of the grave. She removed her coat, folded it neatly, hung it over her husband's stone. She thought of her son, Cary, and her daughter, Andie. Helena fumbled in her pants pockets, withdrew the rosary that Cary, when he was twelve, had given her for Christmas. Andie had sat with chocolate at the corner of her mouth, her husband knelt by the glowing tree, and Cary stood with the cross cupped in his hands. The bounty of presents, nearly all purchased and wrapped by Helena herself, had lain at their feet. With her knee brushing her husband's headstone, Helena Burbank wrapped the rosary around her wrist, delved in her pockets, and found them empty—there was nothing left to give.

In New York City, a station wagon pulled onto Lexington Avenue at 46th Street. Alyssa Swan, in the driver's seat, glanced over her shoulder at her daughter, Katie, in the carseat, and at the cat, Willikers, perched half on Katie's leg.

"Look, Mom," said Katie, "Look it." She had her arms above her head, her nose gnarled, her tongue protruding. Katie Swan had the fine features, the blue eyes, and the straight brown hair of her mother. Willikers, a Russian blue, issued a low mewl. The pure gray fur blended with the car's interior.

"Can't look now, Katie-did." A siren whined over the roar of a bus. The interior of the car smelled of exhaust. Williker's tail swished back and forth, touching Katie's arm. Katie pushed absently at the door handle.

"Willikers says he doesn't like the vet, mom," Katie said.

"Willikers is going anyway." Alyssa Swan reached a hand into the back seat to touch her daughter's knee.

"Willikers is scared." Katie gently tugged on the cat's tail. The glass of the building that lined the street reflected a distorted red station wagon, the chrome of the bumper, the antenna, the side windows.

Alyssa Swan stopped with the traffic. She turned to her daughter.

"Look it, mom," Katie said, "there's us." She pointed toward the reflection in the glass. Willikers perched on top of the seat. The crosswalk just before the bumper streamed with pedestrians. Her mom looked at the glass. Katie thrust herself forward using the door handle. Willikers slipped below Katie's feet, next to the door.

"There, mom, there!"

At the corner of 45th and Lexington, the red side door of the station wagon opened, the cat slipped out, and Katie Swan, unaware, waved to the reflection of her mother.

In the Chrysler building, Cary Burbank crawled through the ventilation system. He wore a blue one-piece worksuit, knee and elbow pads. The cellular phone on his belt scraped against the side of the vent. He pushed a thin toolbox before him. A headlamp, strapped to his head with nylon webbing, lit the dim shaft. He stopped, pulled a letter from his pants pocket—a note from his mother, on stationary printed with canaries and scented of meadowsweets, received in the mail this morning. *Dear Cary,* he reread, *I tire of this house. Remember that children are faultless. I love you so dearly. Your blood fills my heart. Don't worry for me. I'll visit your father's grave. I've always done well enough alone.* He folded and unfolded the letter; then replaced it in his pocket. He shimmied forward. He pushed himself with knees and toes, pulled with hands and elbows. His head occasionally scraped against the top of the vent. He cursed. At intervals he stopped, examined a seam or dent in the ductwork, pulled a notebook from the toolbox, took notes. Coming to a T-shaped intersection, he rubbed his eyes with a thumb and forefinger. He rested. He pulled a ventilation diagram from his breast pocket, flattened it before him, looked at it beneath the light. He turned left. The vent smelled lightly of ozone. He mopped his forehead. He crawled.

The tunnel of the vent was narrow and a-schematic. His headlamp dimly lit the ventway. The path forked before him. Fans of sweat marked his armpits. He flattened the diagram before him, turned it upside down. His hands and knees ached. Ahead in the distance shined horizontal slats of light.

In Chicago, Illinois, on the ninety-first floor of the John Hancock Center, Katie Swan's father, Andrew Swan, a TV repairman, walked down a long corridor. He had just finished a housecall. Identical doorways, white with red trim, lined the hall. Andrew Swan entered the service corridor, which held the cargo elevator. He was preoccupied with thoughts of his distant wife, their separation, his move to Chicago. He thoughtlessly opened the exit to a stairwell and walked rapidly down the first flight of stairs. The steel fire door slammed heavily behind him. He turned. The stairs and walls were poured of featureless concrete. The railing was the color of lemon. A hint of cigarette smoke hung in the air. Andrew Swan stopped halfway between floors. He returned to the door above him. His shoulders were squared beneath his leather coat. In his left hand he held a toolbox. His right hand flexed, reached toward the handle. The door was locked. He was on the ninety-first floor. Andrew Swan's fist pounded against steel.

At the base of the Chrysler Building, Aary Swenson looked upward. A crowd pressed around him. Traffic stalled in the street. The sound of a helicopter passed. A wide thigh grazed Aary Swenson's face, a knee pressed his stomach. He was swept with the crowd, squeezed and pushed by the thickness of bodies. His face was pressed against coats that smelled of tobacco, oranges, vanilla. He looked up: the Chrysler building rising; the reflection of clouds upon glass; the canyon of sky; the gulls. He was tugged in contradictory directions. He stumbled. He reeled. He held to the seam of a stranger's pants.

Andie Hanover née Burbank remained near the table, her mother's note in her hand. Mucus from her nose ran to her lip. Wind whistled past the patio doors. The clock above the stove ticked. The air-blown heat kicked on. Andie Hanover crumpled the note in her hand. She thought of her mother last evening, standing at the oven, stirring the fish stock, slicing celery and onions and carrots on the cutting board, her mother's eyes watering fiercely over the onions. On the couch, Andie had blown her nose, and, rising to walk to the bathroom, she'd stopped to untie her mother's apron strings like she'd done as a child. The air had smelled of oil and salt and potato. Her mother had wiped her hands against the apron, touched Andie's chin. Her mother's pupils held single flickering lights. She had not moved. She had not wiped the water from her eyes. She had not smiled.

On Lexington Avenue, Alyssa and Katie Swan called their cat's name. The red station wagon was double-parked behind them, hazard lights flashing. Ahead, the cat raced along the gutter.

"Willikers," Katie called, "Willikers!"

Willikers stopped, turned his head toward Katie's voice, then toward the crush of people on the sidewalk. A bicycle swerved around him. His tail swished. The slush in the street wet his fur. Alyssa Swan pulled Katie by the hand. Katie's hand trembled. Horns blared. Drivers yelled out their windows. Willikers, scrambling, dashed toward a slow-rolling city bus and then away again.

"Hurry, Katie," Alyssa said. Katie had begun to cry. Willikers ran down Lexington Avenue, his eyes straining wide, his ears flicking—and, jumping among the crowd of legs on the sidewalk, he disappeared.

In the Chrysler building, Cary Burbank took a cordless power screwdriver from his toolbox. Before him, bars of light cut through a ventilation grill. He felt as though the shaft had tightened around him. Cary's hair brushed the top of the shaft, and he recalled his mother lightly touching his head. Sweat ran from his hairline. He removed his gloves.

Cary Burbank's hands looked like his mother's. He thought of how she smelled of cloves. He remembered his mother's hand had once welled with blood. He thought of her on the black and white kitchen tile. Water boiling in a pot on the stove, the kitchen knife on the floor. His sister, Andie, in the doorway. He had stood before his mother, looking up at her. She was impossibly tall. Her hair wreathed her face. She wrung her bleeding hand, looked down at him, told him not to worry, that everything was going to be fine.

He put his gloves back on. He removed the grill to the exhaust vent and held it in his gloved hands.

In the Greek Orthodox Cemetery, Helena Burbank was calm. Light clouds massed in the sky. The snow beneath her feet radiated cold. She thought of all she would miss. Chamomile tea. Buttermilk biscuits. Homemade jam. The quiet of early mornings. The smell of the earth in her tomato garden. The shuddering half-breaths of a baby beginning to cry. The orange light of fall evenings. The chance to knit her grandchildren scarves and mittens. Making them turkey soup. Her children, Cary and Andie—their freckles and scars. Their foolishness and generosity. Her children. Her children making her laugh.

Helena Burbank cocked her head, listening. There was nothing. Distantly, a thousand starlings swarmed the sky. She took the knife from her husband's headstone and drove the blade quickly into her abdomen and up toward her heart.

In the John Hancock Center, on the seventy-fifth floor stairwell, Andrew Swan paused. In his mind he held the image of his daughter walking slowly next to him—her step light and quick; her hand grasping his arm; her eyes flickering down the stairs; her weight supported by his own. Andrew Swan's right hand ran along the handrail.

Each door between the ninety-first floor and the seventy-fifth floor had been locked. The door at the seventy-fifth floor bore the number 75 in black. Andrew Swan's legs had begun to ache. Each floor, but for the number, looked identical. He imagined sitting at the dinner table in New York with his wife and daughter, telling them how he'd locked himself in a stairwell—he thought of his daughter's crooked smile, his wife's gentle laugh. He shifted his toolbox from the left hand to the right. With seventy-four floors beneath him, Andrew Swan estimated that there were 2,670 stairs between him and the ground. He put each foot below the next. The shade of the concrete walls reminded him of his wife's skin.

A rectangle of light opened before Cary Burbank. He put the grill aside, felt the shear of the wind, and—craning his head forward—looked down. He was seventy floors above the ground. He pulled his head back, breathed deeply, looked again. The light blinded him momentarily. Then, beneath him lay Lexington Avenue. Finger-length cars sat idle in the road. Hundreds of people milled on the sidewalks. Cary Burbank watched the reds, the blacks, the greens and blues of their winter coats; the windblown scarves like tails; the dots of colored hats. He felt dizzy. The world beneath him spun. He shook his head. Sweat ran down his temple, curved across his jawline, beaded on his chin, and hung above the wide swath of space below.

Cary Burbank thought of his mother's note. He had never known what his mother had meant. Why had she made Red Velvet cake for her birthdays? Why, even as she aged, wouldn't she wear makeup? Why never utter a curse? Why wear such colors as she wore, the purples and greens and reds?

In New York City, seven hundred feet above ground level, a single droplet of sweat, tear-shaped and opalescent, quivered and then fell.

Alyssa and Katie Swan ran along the side of Lexington Avenue. Ahead, they caught glimpses of the gray cat between cars, beside a payphone, atop a manhole.

"I see him!" Katie called. Her mother held her hand.

The cat moved forward faster than they did. Cars honked as they pass. People called from the street.

"Willikers!" Katie yelled. Alyssa Swan headed toward the payphone ahead. She had lost hope. But as they ran forward, they kept yelling his name.

Beside the Chrysler building, tall crowds parted roughly around Aary Swenson. Legs swept by him. He was jostled, nestled, pressed against a mailbox. His Burberry plaid scarf, tied by his father, had come undone. His corduroy coat was a size too large. His eyes were dark and damp like earth. Aary Swenson looked up at the Chrysler building, upon the lower panes of glass and the lights floating behind them, the panels leading upward; the reflections of the buildings behind him; the shining art deco gargoyles at cornices; and then higher, rising—as his father felt that the mitten was empty, turned wildly, pushed against the crowd—to the welded scrollwork, the gentle metallic slope, which itself again rose, exclamation-like. Aary Swenson saw the small glowing sphere of a face leaning far over some high ledge, and then—as his father's arms snatched him from against the mailbox and held him, tight and shivering—he wondered what face he had seen in the sky.

In the John Hancock Center, Andrew Swan had stopped paying attention to the numbers of the floors. He was dizzy. He moved downward. At the bottom of the stairs, he found a concrete room with the steel door locked. He was underground. Buried, Andrew thought. He thought of his wife and daughter in New York, their similar pear-like smell, their skin. Andrew Swan raised his fist to drum against the steel door. A lightbulb hung, like a tear, from the ceiling by a cord.

Beside the Chrysler building, a drop of sweat fell floor after floor— the surface revolving and prismatic with oil—cleaving through air, absorbing dust motes, winking by lighted windows. The shape was inconstant: stretching and flattening; buffeted by layers of air; driven by gravities and winds; nearly disintegrating to a thousand droplets but holding, cohering, racing into that plummet below.

In Woodstock, Illinois, Andie Hanover née Burbank picked up the phone. Her hands shook. The skin of her face flushed. The note from her mother dropped to the floor. She rapidly dialed the number of her brother. She remembered the phone ringing, in the past; ringing in the kitchen as her brother, eight years old with unfocused brown eyes, had stood beside their mother in the kitchen, his arms upraised while her mother's eyebrows arched wide and her face whitened as blood welled from the cut in her hand. Her cupped palm faced upwards. Blood collected on the knuckle of her pinky, strained, and dripped to the white floor. A kitchen knife clattered. Her brother's lower lip had trembled.

Andie Hanover's bare feet absorbed the chill of the tile. Her bathrobe fell half open. As she dialed, the tones sounded tinny and bright. The number that stood for her brother had never felt so long. She pressed the phone to her ear, trembled so hard she nearly dropped the phone, and waited while the phone rang.

IN THE HANCOCK CENTER, Andrew Swan—locked in the concrete stairwell with the faint smell of mildew, the deep-felt hum of unseen machinery, the single light above—sat shaking on a stair. He put his head against his knees.

AT LEXINGTON AND 42ⁿᵈ, Aary Swenson—nestled in his father's arms—felt the impact of a drop against his forehead. The feeling was momentary and cold. A chill ran through him. His father tightened his grip. Aary Swenson turned his head from the heights above him, toward the street, toward the gray cat that darted past the wheel of the 4-by-4, slipped under the taxi, stepped away from the motorcycle, froze before the advance of the limousine.

IN THE GREEK ORTHODOX CEMETERY, Helena Burbank lay with her face against the snowy earth. Her coat, hanging over her husband's stone, flapped in the wind. The back of her gray dress cut low. Skeletal trees quivered. The knife lay beneath her. Her fingers scratched against the ground. Her blood melted the snow.

At the corner of Lexington and 43rd, Alyssa and Katie Swan were surrounded by pedestrians. They stood beside the payphone. Alyssa dialed. Willikers was nowhere to be found. Wind whistled down the street. Alyssa cradled the phone between her cheek and her shoulder. She held her daughter's face to her chest as she cried.

Above New York City, Cary Burbank's cellular phone began to ring. A gust of wind caused his hair to flock. Pigeons reeled in the air. Cary Burbank pulled his head back in the vent, lifted his phone, and strained to hear—over the rush of wind—the voice on the other side.

A Night Choral

My name is Julianne Kinsman. Early this morning, while my daughter slept on the living room couch, I drew a bath. There was an hour of dark before sunrise, and, in the dim light, the walls of the bathroom were a visceral maroon. My chest was beaded with sweat. With the faucet running, I lowered my legs into the tub, and my shins appeared to bend as they passed from the air to the water. This was re-fraction: the bending of light as it moves from one medium to another. Fully immersed, my knees poked above the surface of the water, and my calves looked broken, and my hands trembled when I unknotted my hair.

Through the window, the sky was pockmarked with dwindling stars, those distant epicentra, emitting energy. Steam rose over the sides of the tub and sunk to the floor. I teach seventh grade astronomy, and—in spite of distractions such as the quake of hands and the unnatural bend of legs—I knew that the name for luminous energy is light.

I imagined getting out of the bathtub naked, and going, still dripping, to kneel beside my daughter on the couch. I imagined shaking her gently awake. I imagined what it would be like as we began to talk, and I imag-ined the dark trail of water that I'd leave behind on the beige carpet.

Hot water ululated through the faucet, and my hands balanced on my knees. I stayed put, safe in the tub.

JUST BEFORE MIDNIGHT last night, my daughter had drifted off on the couch, one of her hands trailing over the edge as if pointing toward the piano. Her yellow quilt looped around her head. Only an angled nose remained; a pink cheek bisected by a strand of black hair. I was getting ready for bed, listening to the branches of our sycamores rattle in the wind, and the air whistled in the chimney flue.

The phone rang with the exigency that sharp sounds have only late at night.

The house was dark except for the cone of light from the lamp in the dining room and the nightlight in the bathroom. I tiptoed in socks and answered quickly so my daughter would not wake. I put the phone to my ear. Outside, the clouds looked bluish with moonlight. A few stars showed through gaps in the clouds. The names of the stars were Sualocin, Rotanev, and Dened Dulfim. In the glass doors leading to the back porch, I looked at myself in the mirror: a long, angled face; thick eyebrows and lips; wisps of hair like feathers at my cheeks; the phone nestled to my ear.

On the line was my ex-husband's sister, Meredith.

"Julianne?" a woman's voice said. "It's Meredith. He's died."

I had not seen or spoken with Meredith, or my ex-husband Phillip, since the first year of my daughter's life, sixteen years ago. "Hold on. Meredith? Who's died?"

"He's dead, Julianne."

"Meredith, I haven't talked to you in ages." I opened the glass doors to the back porch and stepped outside. The cold night air stung like nettles.

"He drove his car into a lake."

"Who? Phillip?" The night sky rippled with distant light.

"He drowned," she said.

"He's dead? *Phillip's* dead?"

"Yes, he's dead," she said.

I hung up the phone.

At Woodrow Wilson Jr. High, I have taught Astronomy to seventh and eighth grade students for nearly fifteen years. Anymore, this span of time doesn't feel so long. Within the tenure of my life, every new year has shortened as if each successive minute was infinitesimally smaller than the last. Consequently, I don't find measurements useful. Units of time, minutes and days and years, are only names that separate my memories— the red-hued wail of my daughter, new born; my ex-husband grinning, one-sidedly, down at her in my arms; the bloody yellow quilt around my daughter and, outside, the leafless sycamore branches outlined by sun— from my present-day peculiarities. In tangible ways, the past remains: the yellow quilt that once wrapped around my daughter now lays on my daughter's bed; the sycamores, though their branches arch closer to the sky, still lose their leaves come winter; and, though my ex-husband has passed away, my daughter wears his one-sided grin.

Let me admit that I have never believed that the dead are entirely gone. There's no evidence for this—it's absurd. Yet the light from distant suns takes years to reach our eyes on earth, and the stars we see above us are decades or even centuries old. And so the night sky, which cups above us, is a vision of a past we've never known.

Raising my leg from the water and watching it unbend, I lathered it with soap. The razor felt sharp enough to part an object from its name. Goosebumps rose. I refused to cry. Each hair on my leg cut with a minor tug. What happened to a name, like Phillip, when the thing that it once stood for had ceased to exist? Grains of leg hair rode on the water's surface tension. Steam swirled over the tub. The mirror above the sink ran with condensation. Outside the bathroom door, my daughter slept.

Like a pulse beneath skin, I could sense that, even in sleep, she waited for an explanation that I did not have.

What could I tell her? That when we were young, Phillip, my ex-hus-

band, liked tequila? I did, too. When we were drinking together, he sometimes wore a cashmere scarf that once belonged to his grandmother?
When he raised his glass to his mouth, he exposed the tattoo of a dove on
his arm?

Phillip won't drink tequila any more. That scarf might still exist, I don't
know. Would it be right to say that he no longer has the tattoo? Can I say
that those names—the tattoo; the scarf; the tequila—now have him?

From the tub, I heard my daughter's footsteps. She was awake so early!
There was so much that I ought to have told her long ago; such a horrible
thing that I needed to tell her now. The sound of her steps transitioned
from the living room rug, to hardwood, to the tile of the kitchen. The
tub water eddied around my skin. My wet hair felt cold against my neck.
Sualocin, Rotanev, and Dened Dulfim, the stars visible through the
bathroom window, formed the constellation named Delphinus.

When I blinked, my eyelids felt grainy and abrasive. The tub water had
gone cold. I imagined the rush of light from the stars travelling through
the vacuum of space to enter the earth's atmosphere. The light from a distant galaxy refracts, bends—like legs entering the tub—as it passes through
vacuums, gas belts, galaxies. What we finally see is bent and transformed.
The stars are purloined by the space that intervenes.

My daughter's footsteps returned from the kitchen to the living room.
The piano bench creaked with her weight. The keylid flipped and slid. The
reflection of the moon burned in the bathroom mirror. She played Aaron
Copland's *The Cat and the Mouse* with the soft pedal pressed the whole
time. My daughter, Lillian.

In Chicago, Phillip and I had taught each other how to drink. We'd lined
up glasses of tequila and spoke, on my part, of the composition of the
heavens, and, on his, of the imagined hills and sands of far-off places, of
the people in Transdanubia in the Republic of Hungary, or of Mt. Mold-
oveanu in Transylvania. He had not traveled but had studied the names

of places and of things. He could name parts of my body that I had never considered—the first night we met, he touched my lips with a finger and called the vertical groove above my upper lip a *philtrum*. At our second dinner, he touched the bump on the back of my head and named it a *nunion*. A few weeks later, he told me that *Mongomery's tubercles* was the name for the tiny bumps on the areolae of my nipples.

A black hole can be formed when a massive star, a supernova, collapses under its own gravity. Two hundred and fifty million lightyears away, in the Perseus galaxy cluster, ripples in the hot gas surrounding a supermassive black hole revealed themselves—to the astronomer's eye—as sound waves. This galaxy played a single note. Constant yet inaudible, the note corresponded to a B-flat, fifty-seven octaves below middle-C on the piano. This sound is believed to have existed for two and a half billion years.

THE PIANO BENCH creaked as my daughter shifted. She played Beethoven's *Moonlight Sonata*. Getting out of the tub, I pulled on a robe and opened the bathroom door. The pale yellow of the living room walls caught and held the light from the twin table lamps. Her back was to me. She wore all black. Her hands—in their flow and halt and crawl—addressed the shape of our lives. Her hair was as dark as the black lacquered wood of the piano; her skin very white.

She had never really met her father. After Lillian was born, Phillip had moved out, following the cocktail world, the late nights, and the hunger for names he didn't know. When I was able, I moved Lillian to the distant suburbs where we live now.

When I walked across the room, trailing my hand along the back of our old leather couch, my daughter did not look at me. The kitchen door's hinges squealed as I pushed past. I picked up the phone, and dialed my ex-husband's sister, Meredith.

"Meredith," I said. "What happened?"

"I told you. He drove into a lake."

"A lake? What lake?"

"It's called Skaneateles."

"Where in the world is that? Were you with him?"

"Jesus, Julianne, not in the car."

"After, I mean?"

"I saw him."

"Were you…was he? In pain, I mean. You know. Did he look all right?"

"He was dead. He looked fucking awful."

"I haven't talked to Phillip in fifteen years."

"Goddamn it, Julianne."

"Fuck you, Meredith." I hung up the phone again.

Just after we first met, I took Phillip out to a cornfield. I showed him the flashy planets: the moons of Jupiter; the ice rings of Saturn. I avoided the more intricate explanations: not mentioning the hour it took light to pass between Jupiter and earth, nor that Saturn's rings are mainly composed of ice, nor that Jupiter's unobservable ring system is made of dust from interplanetary meteoroids crashing against the planet's moons. I held Phillip around the waist as he peered blindly into the telescope at Saturn's rings. Then, as he studied the moon, I told of Jupiter's flattened main ring, and the inner cloud-like ring, called the halo. We can't see Jupiter's rings, I said. The faint third ring, which really consisted of two rings, one embedded inside the other, was named, because of its transparency, the gossamer ring.

From the living room, Lillian called my name. Outside the kitchen windows, the morning sky remained dark. She had stopped playing the piano. "Who were you talking to?" she asked.

"No one," I said. From the hanging basket beside the stove, I took two brown pears. I walked into the living room. Lillian sat on the piano bench. Her hair hung in dark strands across her face; her silver earrings dangled. She wore six silver rings.

Lillian will only remember her father through photos. We have only two displayed around the house, more in the closet. In the living room, we keep a black-and-white photo of Phillip in a suit and tie. A face as sculpted as plasterwork; a hat in his hands; full light striking his left side. In Lillian's room, on her desk, she keeps a photo of Philip painting the living room walls. He stands on a ladder as if it's a plinth. He's shirtless. He's streaked with white housepaint and holds a brush in one hand. His head turns toward the camera, and his smile, probative and toothy, seems to hold all the reasons that I once loved him.

Handing Lillian a pear, I brushed my hand against her back. My face felt hot. Phillip, in his suit-and-tie photo on the end table, faced us. The two table lamps flickered as the refrigerator kicked on. My daughter, staring at the piano keys, shook her head. My chest tightened as I tried to speak, but she spoke first.

"I feel this sort of panic, Mom," she said. Her pursed lips looked serious. Her eyes were open and as watery as when she was apologizing. "I don't know why it happened."

I said, "Something's happened?"

"It wasn't me who broke the window." She set her pear on the piano.

"One of our windows?" I asked.

"Not our window," she said. "A store window."

"So you've broken a store's window. Not such a big deal. What store?"

"It was last night, Mom."

"Was it a big window?"

"You don't know the people I was with. It was a bakery window. I don't remember the name."

"Why would anyone want to break the window of a bakery?"

"We didn't steal anything."

"You have to tell me you're *not* stealing things?"

Exoterically, the stars we see are fixed: we develop star charts, and link patterns of stars into constellations that represent sea monsters, a swordfish, a phoenix, serpents, bears, chameleons. At forty-one years old, while

I struggled to tell Lillian that her dad was dead, it occurred to me that we, like the constellations, were collections of unrelated points held together, arbitrarily, by nomenclature.

It was Phillip who named our daughter Lillian. As a child, Lillian kept a chameleon named Milhous in a terrarium. He lived for a short while, and then he died. In death, Milhous turned a dull gray-brown. We held a ceremony. We buried him at the base of the bloodroot bush near a back window, and over his grave we laid the largest rock we could lift.

My daughter, now sixteen, wears almost exclusively black or gray. She wears eyeliner, lipstick in shades of dark red and purple.

"How did this window get broken exactly?" I asked.

"We were just talking, Mom." She was uncomfortable. Her hands fidgeted. She didn't look me in the eyes.

"Conversation pretty much never breaks glass."

"We were talking about Kevin Wong. He's got leukemia, Mom. He's got no hair. He misses a lot of school. He wears a hat." Light glittered in points on the polish of the piano.

"This Kevin—he's dying?"

"That's what we were saying." Lillian ran one hand across the piano. "I mean that's what I was saying—that Kevin was dying. That soon he'd be dead."

"So you broke a window? You thought this would do some good?"

Esoterically, I wanted to say, the stars as we see them are products of the mediums through which light must pass. Including, it seemed clear to me, *us*, our corneas and irises, our measures of time, our losses and lives.

"I told you I didn't break the window, Mom," she said. "Goddamn. We were upset."

When Phillip and I moved in together, we lived in a studio apartment on Chicago's north side. The apartment was just a medium-sized main room and a closet-sized bathroom. The walls had yellowed with the smoke of past occupants, and the air smelled of boiled pork. We had nothing really: a dresser picked off the curb, a left-behind floor lamp, an old farm table, a mattress. Neither of us were yet comfortable with the other's skin. The bathroom provided the only moments of privacy. The bed was lumpy; the light from the single lamp too dim. We yelled a lot. I argued that we ought to root ourselves, find work, dedicate ourselves to whatever deserved our dedication. In the evenings, I took the Chevy out of the city and into the fields, speculated over deviations in the night sky. Phillip wanted names his mouth could scarcely shape. Addis Ababa in Ethiopia. Campinas in Brazil. He rode the El toward the bright lights of bars and nightclubs, and, when he returned, he repeated the names of men and women he'd met.

We were both glad for the separation. We found each other refractory. At his slightest touch, I shrugged, turned my head, scowled. He'd tell me, in his graveling voice, that the majority of the nodules on the surface of the tongue were named *filiform papillae*, or that the medical name for a birthmark, like the peanut-shaped blotch on the inside of my thigh, was a *nevus*. Then he would step outside, walk toward the train station, and not return for two days. Slowly, that which used to seem determinate of my world—the starveling, hollow cheeks; a finger against my divisible lips; the revelation of my body's names—came to be quotidian. What appeared at first as a ring of light, a halo, a star-crossed phenomenon of prevenient grace, turned out, under the pressure of time and space, to be nothing more than dust.

Sitting on the piano bench, Lillian leaned back against me. Her fingers flirted over the keys. When had she gotten dark rings beneath her eyes? Morning hadn't risen yet. In the corners of the room, shadows gathered into impenetrability. Out the window, the interstellar spaces were still a deep black. The silhouettes of sycamore trees branched below the stars. All of this reminded me of what my daughter did not know. Of what I needed to tell her.

"So we were walking along the sidewalk," she said. "Mom, are you listening?"

"Of course, I'm listening. What else?"

"On the sidewalk, by the bakery," she said. She leaned harder against me. A strand of her hair brushed my neck. "Suzy and Marilyn were talking about how Kevin didn't have hair. Brian was looking at himself in the reflection of the bakery's window. He was saying he didn't like Kevin anyway. He's narcissistic, mom. He's got a hooked nose. And a scar by one ear."

"A hooked nose? Like a bird?"

"I told Brian that he was an asshole. That he was going to die, too."

"Oh, good. Good! People like that," I said.

"Then Brian threw a rock through the window."

The name of the type of rock we placed over Milhous's grave was basalt. We stood above the grave; our arms hung at our sides; my daughter held my hand. Her face was a miniature of mine. The sun had yellowed and dried the grass of our lawn. For the first time in Milhous death, Lillian had seen the dissolution of something fragile. She kicked the rock over the grave. Basalt forms on faultlines where the earth's tectonic plates separate or diverge. I told my daughter that things break apart. From the fissure, I said, new things emerge. Lillian was eight years old; she didn't find words very comforting. She didn't know the meaning of *fissure*.

"Then we ran away," Lillian said, "to the park, and Brian started kissing me." Under the soft lamplight, the brown pear on the piano looked like a still life. Delphinus, the constellation visible through the bay window, included the stars Sualocin and Rotenev. Suolocin spelled backwards is Nicolaus. Rotenev is Venetor. Nicolaus Venetor was a 19th Century Italian astronomer. Rotenev is ninety-seven light years away. The light that we see from Rotenev is nearly a century old.

"Didn't his hooked nose get in the way of the kissing? And didn't you say something about scarring?"

"He's cute, Mom."

"Cute *scarring*?—that's why you two started kissing?"

"It was my first real kiss, Mom. I don't know why. We were sort of depressed."

I should have told Lillian how her father's voice, on the day she was born, sounded low and quavering like the rumble of moving earth. He'd held her awkwardly in front of him in two cupped hands, and he couldn't stop looking at her, touching her skin, putting her fingers to his teeth. What I should have told her was that the galaxies swirling above us are choral. Or that our trajectories on this earthy landscape are free and clear. I should have told her the sweeter stories of her father—how his long hair tucked behind his ears in sigmoid curves; how on an early date he'd given me roadside sunflowers in a bucket; how for the first week of her life he'd carried her at his side, not wanting to put her down.

"Did you ever think," I said, "of how the earth beneath this house is composed of dead things?"

"God, Mom!" Lillian said. "That's weird." She ran her hands across the piano's keys. She mentioned names of people at school: Kevin Wong, Susan Fairbanks, Marilyn Noonan. There I stood, just behind her; she just before me.

Lillian got up, pushed the piano bench out, and walked into the kitchen. She stood before the dirty dishes in the sink; she turned the hot water on, picked up the soap. She said she felt unimportant.

"Right now," she said, "I feel like there's just my name, Lillian. There's a broken window. I don't really have any real friends."

"Is this what they're teaching you?"

"No one's teaching me anything."

"Good," I say, "that's good." We were quiet for a minute. The sink had filled with water. Her hands cupped a bowl. "So who's this Susan?" I asked.

"She's got this hair, Mom. It looks like a fur hat."

"And Marilyn?"

"I don't know—she's pretty. She bats her eyelids. She likes cartoons."

"They sound fine, these people."

"I don't think they like me."

I watched her lift dishes. The curve of her back; her hands recursively entering the water; the uplift of her forearms. The shimmer of refluent water trailed across her skin. The dishrag swirled over the lips of glasses, the back of plates. Her hands bent as they entered the water and unbent as she drew them out.

"I'm so tired of this, Mom." There was no irony, no humor. She wore a cheap silver necklace in the shape of the sun. Her earrings dangled like tinsel. The yellow flowers of the bloodroot bush pressed against the window.

"The dishwashing?"

"It's hard, Mom. I'm not like you."

My daughter saw me, connected the lines on my face to the scars, and labeled me as old. Her friends and acquaintances fit into discrete groups. Hair ought to look a certain sculpted way; eyebrows must be thin; legs must be elongated and waxed. She was so certain of the rules in her social world. I wanted to tell her that only uncertainty grows.

At dinner once, my drunk ex-husband grabbed the fork off my plate and threw it out the window. I was nine months pregnant. We'd been trying to discuss what a child might need in terms of parenting, what changes our life might have to undergo. The light of the candle on the table flickered some unknown code. Phillip threw my fork and looked at me defiantly. My underarms were dampened by ovals of sweat, but I finished eating my broiled salmon and sweet potato with my fingers. Later that night, when I stepped outside to retrieve my fork, I found it sticking upright in a patch of dirt. The heavens stirred above me, and, looking down at that fork, I knew, at last, the obvious: the three of us would not work.

"What are you upset about?" I asked my daughter.

"I'm not sure," she said.

The name of the star closest to the earth is Proxima Centauri. Proxima Centauri is part of a triple star system. The other two stars, Alpha Centauri A and B, orbit one another. Two small scars above Lillian's left eyebrow tell the story of how she ran away, slept in a culvert, came home bedraggled and bleeding. The scar on her chin comes from my ex-husband, on the checkered tile of the kitchen, drunkenly letting Lillian, at five-months old, roll off the table.

I poured myself lemonade, added some tequila, and called Meredith again. Lillian held a blue plate before her in both hands. The door between the living room and kitchen swung shut behind me. I went into the bathroom and sat on the toilet.

"Quit hanging up on me," Meredith said.

"Maybe," I said. "I called to talk this time."

"Okay then. Go on."

"I don't know what I feel about this, Meredith. Do you?"

"Not really."

"He never knew his daughter," I said.

"He might have wanted to."

"Jesus, it's been sixteen years. Except for in the beginning, I hardly thought of him."

"He wasn't well, really. I don't think he was ever well."

"I wanted him so badly once," I said.

I imagined my ex-husband, Phillip Kinsman, sitting in our old, rusted Chevy beside lake Skaneateles. I don't know where this lake is, but Phillip looked as he did sixteen years ago. He wore a gray flannel shirt that I'd given him when we were twenty. It was dark. The car's nose tilted toward the water. The headlights were on. Wheel ruts led back toward a road. The Chevy's windows were down. Did Phillip's hand shake as he put the car in neutral? The car slowed as it enters the water. Phillip's mouth was open. The headlights submerged. The water looked gritty and gray, and it lapped at the windshield. The side windows let the water in. Phillip's face glowed lightly. He held the steering wheel. His seatbelt was fastened tight. The water rose to his chest, his neck, his divided lips. Did he hold his breath?

In the kitchen, the rattling of dishes stopped. The door of the refrigerator thumped open. Meredith and I both held silently to the open phone line.

"I've got to go, Meredith," I said. "I need to speak with my daughter."

"All right," she said, "Goodbye, Julianne."

"Goodbye," I said.

Lillian returned to the piano. She played Joplin's *The Entertainer*. Her black hair sat softly on her shoulders. Her eyes were half closed and one eyebrow raised slightly. She is perfectly beautiful, and I told her so.

"Your dad," I said. Outside of the windows, the slightest glimmer of light had risen in the east. Lillian did not stop playing the piano. "I half carried him once," I said. "Home from a bar, in a blackout. He was so damn heavy. I got us in a taxi, got him home to bed."

My daughter fingers stopped moving on the piano. She looked at me and did not look away. But I turned, walked to the hall closet, put an old wool coat over my robe, grabbed a few pictures of Phillip out of a box, and put them in a pocket.

In a black hole, gravity is so strong that the escape velocity exceeds the speed of light. Nothing can escape. Does Lillian know that a black hole is formed when a large star, a supernova with a maximum intrinsic luminosity one billion times that of the sun, collapses? We see only the outward explosion of the supernova, which masks the implosion going on inside.

"Mom," my daughter called, "are you all right?" She left the piano and walked up behind me in the hall. She saw me wearing the coat. "Where're you going?"

"Come outside with me a minute," I said.

It is never truly quiet or dark at night. There is a muted refulgence. Stars, which I won't name, spattered the sky in patterns that have taken me years to see. Each star marked a solar system as discrete and complex as our own. The distance between each was unbridgeable. Birds had begun to call from the triangular hulk of the fir tree, the rounded holly bush, the reaching sycamores. Above us, the galaxies hummed. My daughter stood a few feet away from me, but the distance between us felt interminable.

"I need to talk to you," I told her. My hand felt the photos of Phillip in my coat pocket.

"Okay."

I said, "I'm going to cry."

"Don't, Mom," she said. She looked at me. Above her, Alpha Centauri shone.

"This is about your father," I said. Her hands dangled lightly at her sides. The whole sky had begun to glow. I said my daughter's name. My hands shook, but I reached out.

In a moment, I would tell her about her dad, but I needed her to understand that the distance between us is named space. The units of distance have been named miles, lightyears, inches, feet. Light can travel the distance between Alpha Centauri and our place on this earth in roughly four-and-a-half years. The human organ of sight is named an eye. The eye can be opened, or closed; the eye can adjust to light and estimate distances. An upper limb of the human body is named an arm. The grassy space between my daughter and me can be measured in feet. The arm can extend, can bridge space, can travel units of distance like lightyears or feet to grasp onto a name, like Lillian, and pull it close to our side.

Cosmology

Six years ago your mom and I met in the shadow of the granite dome of the state capital building in Madison, Wisconsin. Her hair was a coppery brown and her skin white like a girl who spent her time indoors. I held out the text from my night class in astronomy called *The Evolving Universe: Stars, Galaxies, and Cosmology,* and she looked back at me and she said her name was Madeleine and asked if I wanted to get a cup of coffee. I said that I didn't drink coffee but that I would like to get a cup of coffee.

In a brown-and-pink painted café, we drank a brew so bitter it made my jaw ache and my brow wrinkle, but Madeleine smiled and I said that I was looking for someone to meet for a supper of green beans and crêpes, and for afternoon deli sandwiches and glasses of wine, and at neighborhood chrome-and-neon diners to breakfast on grapefruit and French toast, and eventually learn the names of the waitstaff, and we'd talk the big talk about what shape the future held (at the moment I envisioned it as a doughnut) and how the same old cornfield could look entirely different under heavy pre-storm light or the rusty orange of sunset or cold blue lamplight, and we'd talk about the thousands of lights we'd seen and those we couldn't yet imagine, and how I have a memory of my mother prior to her death carrying a basket of kale, and how a halo of light hovers over Chicago at night, and how in a kiss one could transmit not only lust but a desire to give oneself over to a better world as represented by another—maybe by her—by Madeleine and as such this wasn't something to be entered into lightly.

Madeleine chewed her chocolate cruller with her mouth half open and her dusky hair hung in her face and her shoulders shook like she might begin laughing. But she didn't. She said she wanted someone who wasn't afraid to take chances like diving off a high board even though he hated swimming, or to skinny dip in the neighbor's pool while high-volume listening to Bonnie "Prince" Billy on scratchy speakers. She wanted someone who she could sometimes call *Sunshine* without any sense of irony, and who cried when he discovered that in one of her dresser drawers lay an egret feather and a bit of lace inherited from her grandmother, and someone who when she had god-forbid died wrote letters that went on not about abject misery and insulation but about what a grand time they'd had, and someone who didn't bitch that she drank way more wine than one really ought to drink, and who wanted to share with her every tidbit—not just the last few cherries in the fridge, but the times and frequency with which they masturbated alone and their favorite words like *crescent* or *serendipity* or *vulva,* and the things in their past they were ashamed of like the time Madeleine had told her mother that she hoped she'd die like a plant left unwatered—until in rare moments they felt as though they'd fused to become a single creature that swallowed each cherry with a single esophagus and chewed with a single set of teeth.

Her main reservation about me, Thom, was that nearly everybody knew the future wasn't a doughnut—which was a silly anus shape—but more of a corkscrew.

We went on talking and meeting after her Master in Education classes until she became the more adventurous of us and kissed me, and we moved into a single apartment that we decorated with cheap sidewalk-found furniture and bundles of unopened daffodils we could get two for a dollar, and every morning in those days I woke up a bit before Madeleine and pulled the patterned sheets tight around us and nudged her awake.

Look at you. So small and new and undefined. Your chin quivers. Your eyes are only open momentarily. Then they are closed. Then open. Then closed.

A few months after we moved in together I brought Maddy to my father's house outside Madison, but I didn't call to tell him we were coming. They hadn't met before, though I'd told dad a lot about her. The house where I was born sits alongside a creek. When we pulled up the sun shone through the pines around the water, and we found my dad in the backyard sitting on a lawn chair. He wasn't wearing a shirt and he looked too thin. No one knew about his lymphoma yet, or that he would die within the next few years. June bugs buzzed among the trees. My dad was a big man and his eyes had a kind of gentle authority. He didn't rise, but looked up at us and said, Madeleine? and he spoke slowly as though he were turning the word around in his mouth. He asked her what her last name was, and she said, Cavanaugh, and he smiled and pushed back his long hair and said, You know that means *chubby*? A smile cracked on his face in the way that a maul splits wood, and his laugh was a low bark until he bent over and began coughing into his hand. When he straightened back up, he asked us if we wanted a beer.

Nothing especially remarkable happened on that visit to my father's house, but I remember the way that my dad glanced at Maddy sideways, and how he sat on the couch and said, Come sit over here by me, and he asked her questions about where she was raised, and how she got along with her parents, and what age of children she wanted to teach. I could tell he liked her, and it felt good. He cooked sausage and spinach for dinner, and he found a bottle of wine in the basement. He said to Maddy, Would you like a glass? and she said, Yes, and he said, I don't drink much wine, and he poured her a glass of cabernet and himself a bourbon. Later he said, What did he tell you about his mother? and Maddy said, He said she cursed at him, and my father said, She did more than that. They eyed one another a little bit territorially as if each thought the other might know things about me that the other did not. My father shrugged his shoulders. He said, I remember once I came home from the General Store where I worked, and I heard Thom crying when I stood at the front door with my keys. Maddy turned and looked at me. I didn't look away. My father said, He was nine years old. He said, They were in the bathroom and she was in there burning his forearm with a wooden match.

What exactly can be taught? What can be passed along from one person to the next? What if there is no grand arc and no sense of scale and no sustained trajectory? What if life does not cohere in the way that I've always believed that it should?

A few months after Maddy met my father, nothing had really changed. For us the world was still the sum of its better parts. Maddy and I were in college, and Maddy would stay up late studying for classes with names like *Seminar on Interpretive Discussion* or *The Gifted: Differentiating Instruction from an Advanced Perspective,* and she held her nose inches from the pages, and I'd make her a cup of tea or a tuna fish sandwich and then coffee before I'd start to fall asleep on the couch watching her—dark hair tied behind her head, and eyelids half drooped, and a hand occasionally pinching her own thigh—and she'd say, Don't go! and she'd throw a pillow at me and say she wanted someone who stuck with her through good sleep and bad, and she'd try to keep me awake with promises of making it up to me and making half-joking come-hither motions with her tongue and then deferring them with an upraised palm. Sometimes she raised her head and her eyes were like lamps and she said, It turns out that you're supposed to talk to your children all the time, and she said, What was wrong with my parents? Or she said, Do you think your mother was nuts? and she said, You know it's a kind of abuse to have a crazy parent in the house? She read and read and it seemed to take hours until her eyes squeezed closed and not another single word could fit through. She lay there limply. She said, Let's get up. She said, Let's do something.

Once I remember mustering the last of my energy, and I said, Okay, and then I said, You asked for it, and I called my childhood friend Rush, and he drove his truck into Madison and showed up at our apartment and hammered at the door with his palm. Maddy paused before opening the door, and she said, This is a good friend of yours? and I said, My oldest friend. The door shook in the frame. It was late enough that our neighborhood had gone silent. Maddy reached out and the sleeve of her shirt gaped at the wrist and she turned the doorknob slowly until it clicked, and the door flew open and Rush stumbled inside. He wore mud-covered boots and tan Carhartt coveralls. His dark hair looked pasted to his forehead. He looked Maddy up and down. I stood five feet behind Maddy in the hallway. I said, You two are going to need to get along, and then for a minute no one said anything. The air outside smelled spiced. A dog barked. Then Maddy turned and put her arm around Rush's, and she looked up at him and said, Why are all of Thom's friends so dirty? and Rush said, He's got other friends?

Why does time jump forward as though it's alive?

The next moment I can remember must have been three years ago—your mother in a corduroy skirt asking me to square dance at the Wisconsin State Fair. Maddy hadn't square danced since classes in grade school but in a tent with a dirt floor we kicked up our heels, and left only after many dos-a-dos's and a lot of embarrassment, and we walked into the fairground and sweated and made fun of ourselves and looked at baby chicks rising from eggshells behind glass.

Maybe this moment stuck with me because it was one of those times that I started to feel bad about nothing. I thought, then, of how I had a propensity for missing the anniversary of our first date, and how my eyes wandered toward any available cleavage, and how last year her tulips had met my empty forgetful hands. When I lose myself inside a book I tune out the world so completely that everything beyond the page becomes gray and feathery and absolutely silent, and Maddy would speak to me and say, Can you pick me up from the dentist's tomorrow? or she'd say, There's a sharp pain in my stomach, and I wouldn't recognize she spoke until frustration wrinkled her face like an accordion, and her finger poked my neck or shoulder.

On a splintered gray picnic table, we ate a tub of vinegary French fries and a cream puff. A few kids threw darts into yellow paper stars. An old man carried a giant stuffed snake.

Maddy said, I've got no sense of timing, and I said, How come? and Maddy said, I have a sort of question, and I said, Shoot. Maddy said, What would you think about us having a baby?

Sometimes I do not think at all.

Two years ago we got married at an old Illinoisan horse farm in the gardens adjacent to a brick and whitewash colonial. Huge bean pods hung from trellises. We'd arranged purple hydrangeas in an old coalscuttle. We'd invited just Rush and my dad. We hired a Justice of the Peace. Maddy wore brown, and the horses whinnied and reared their heads over split-rail fences. The Justice of the Peace was overweight and wore a white suit. He had a double chin and a low voice. We held onto one another as he spoke the *death do us part*s and we said the *I do*s, and then he waddled down the dirt path toward the parking lot, and the four of us sat beneath a sycamore tree. My dad and Rush wore dark ill-fitted suits, and they'd brought bottles of champagne in brown bags but they'd forgotten glasses. I slipped a brown shoulder strap down over Maddy's arm. My father opened four champagne bottles and passed them around and then Rush and my father lifted their bottles above their heads and said cheers, and their faces—Rush's and my dad's—looked so warm and ruddy and human that I couldn't look at them any longer.

Sometimes I think of a mother's womb. I imagine the spaces between us. The stretch of air. The bed.

When we were first together, and living in Madison, and attending classes—Maddy seriously and me haphazardly—I met a girl in my Astronomy course. What was her name? Doris. Maybe Dorothy. We studied together in her dorm room decorated with posters of the torsos of men, and we walked to class together talking about how we weren't sure we belonged in college, and we sat too close to one another on a night-time car ride to the professor's house to look through his telescope at Saturn or Venus, and I remember every bump in that car ride and how it stung—almost burned—when our thighs jolted against one another. I went home to the apartment I shared with Maddy, and I said nothing. Then walking across campus one day, Dorothy and I ran into Maddy who didn't look away, and didn't walk around us, but stood on the concrete path in our way. Her face looked wind-burned. Her arms were bare. She looked at me. She said, Where're you going? and I said, To class, and she kept looking and I said, Astronomy, and I held up the textbook and she waited a little too long before she said, Really? Then she pushed between us and kept going. I watched her back get smaller. I said to Dorothy or Doris, I've got to go, and she said, What about class? and I trotted after Maddy and started trying to think of some way to apologize.

I wish we did not measure our lives with the hours and minutes that must by their very definition pass. So often I've been awhir and livid with life, but when I hold still this world—and what exists within it—is remarkable to consider.

A FEW MONTHS AGO Maddy and I talked about baby names at a picnic
table on the lakeshore as we ate Rainier cherries, and the early sun tippled
from one side of us. Maddy's face was half in the light and half in shadow,
and she wiped her forehead with a hand and asked when I was going to
get off my duff and take a risk and suggest a few names that I liked. Her
entire body seemed to curl around the plot of her belly. I mentioned that I
wanted piles of books and huge alphabetical lists and she said, Let's start
with *Leo* for the growl of the lion, and I said, Leo's for a dork.

The wind gave a little fake growl as it skimmed across the surface of
Lake Michigan. Various members of a large family at the next two picnic
tables kept exclaiming in Spanish and hugging one another.

Maddy said, How about *Florence* for the way that each of us flowers
once and then fades, or *Rachel* for the lamb and the ewe, or *Barbara* for the
mystery that recedes before us. Or maybe Richard to lend us strength. Or
Dick for short.

I NEED to tell you something. Are you ready to listen?

LESS THAN A MONTH AGO, your mother and I sat on the grass and half-
gazed into the endless gassy whirl that Lake Michigan seems at night but
for the bobbing light on a single buoy. We were talking the way we were
always talking about you, and about what came next in this whirligig life,
and about Maddy's distaste for herself when she giggled like one of her
fourth-grade pupils at words like *suck* or *jug,* and about how our sexual life
was like an unexplored country. The feet of joggers slapped against cement.
In the distance were the low growl and the headlights of a machine we
couldn't see mowing grass in the dark. Just to the west, apartment buildings
jutted upward from the coastline like an enormous exposed spine. Maddy
laid back and rolled to one side and her growing stomach spread out across
the ground, and she said that to attract the hummingbird moth she'd taken

her whole class outside and planted mint and dogwood and purple cone-flower and blackberry and trumpet vine and milkweed. She told me how my general lay-about attitude as a part-time handyman became more and more odd as we left our twenties behind, and as her stomach grew, and how her school kids had decorated her room with construction paper versions of themselves and they looked both sadder and wiser than they actually were and how one of her students—a happy-go-lucky girl named Kacee—had written in her journal about her uncle kissing her on the lips, and how sometimes my voice grated on Maddy's ears like the squeal of a pulley, and how she loved those kids so much that she wouldn't let a single one of them be mishandled, and how they were beautiful little prototypes of the way she wanted us to be. At some point she said my name with my hand tucked in hers. She said, Thom Poole. She said, The clearwing sphinx moth is frequently mistaken for a hummingbird, and I said, When did you learn so much about moths? and she said, My kids at school are pretty into bugs, and she said, I think my heart is a moth, and I said, I think mine's a parrot.

We make such wonderful mistakes.

You and your mother lie in the hospital bed. It is night.

Just down the hall past a nursing cart and through the locked doors a small boy is awake when he ought not to be. The boy plays with a blue felt platypus and a wooden train. On the wheeled nursing cart and under flu-orescence lays the lists of medications for each patient. As though outside time the boy's parents stand outside the locked doors and hold completely still. Two nurses drink coffee at a desk outside your room. Nurses wear white no longer. They dress in any color they choose. They are festive. They wear pink and blue. When I lay my head to your mother's chest, can I hear her heart beat? Can I hear yours? Is her pulse calm and strong? Are you the curl of skin beneath her arms? Will I ever hear you breathe?

The boy outside makes the *choo-choo* sounds of the train. It is too late for the boy to be playing but in this place the hour has ceased to matter. The light is diffuse. Streetlight cuts through the window and across the figure of you and your mother and draws a hazy trapezoid on the floor. The lists of medications are on white paper in small black print that blurs and swarms into recognizable shapes. NITROGLYCERINE 2.6MG TAB and TISSUE PLASMA ACTIVATOR .3MG/KG and COUMADIN 7.5MG TAB. On the other side of the doors, the boy crashes the train into walls and with his mouth makes soft plosive noises. *Phoow. Phoow. Phoow.*

And We Saw Light

Divinity is behind our failures and follies also.
–Ralph Waldo Emerson

WE FEEL THE TREMOR of approach. On the paved road lined by wheat, the boy and dog come. Chained men collect trash among the roadside poppies. The scent of fire. The sky races with clouds. The foretaste of blood hangs in the air. The dog whines and rakes her nails on cement. Against the skyline, a tree burns.

The boy calls himself Gil. He breathes hard. He smells the phantom of blood, of his mother's sweat, of boxelder, of anise and cinnamon, of the smoke of green wood. Gil's thoughts outpace him. Gil sweats. The bloodscent raises images—the stillborn he'd found in the compost, the rotting meat, the decaying child, the spindle arms exposing bone, the maggots, the mulch and feces. The soil of this valley. Gil's stomach reminds him he hasn't had supper. Ham hock and mustard greens. Home lies behind him. The chained men sing in low and graveled voices among the poppies. The dog jerks on her rope. Wine-red droplets thicken on cement. Blood. Bloodtrail leading toward the fire in the tree.

Gil, kneeling on the sidewalk, dips his index finger. Sniffs. Recoils.

—What's it, girl?

Dog doesn't know. She lowers her nose, widens her nostrils, breathes. She's a greyhound; she's a gazehound. She knows she's bigger than the boy. She eats ground. Pulls on her leash.

—C'mon, girl, let's go.

The gazehound drags Gil across the cement. She stops. She licks.

—No, girl, no!

Dog doesn't listen. Dog pants. Points her nose forward. Cocks one front paw. Leans her whole frame. Stiffens.

Boy doesn't listen. He squares his shoulders. Braces his feet. Takes the rope two-handed. Pulls. Pulls her toward.

—Home, girl! Home!

—Think she dead, High?

—Don't much care.

—Yeah. Yeah, fuck 'er.

—We done that already.

We hear her voice as she's walking. Her. She. Journeywoman singing the dirge, the hymn, the plainsong. A heartbeat and its echo along the roadside, a worn-skinned mirage in a blue, lily-printed dress—*yes*, this far-traveled figure whose hand strangles the gunnysack by her side. We hear the sound of bared feet against road. We see the moon rising above fields of wheatgrass. We watch. How long must she walk? Large-bellied and singing. The road rolls with foothills. The winds quarrel with one another. The willows flail and lash. Night bleeds across the sky like ink.

We. We are unbeguiled by time; we are that which casts no shadow; we are without want. We are the dust and stones, and we are the street. We are.

The gunnysack. Coarse-fibered. Wet. The bottom that leaks. The dark ovals that trail in the dirt of the road. We, we who shall know neither the day nor the hour, we watch. To the left, a cemetery; to the right, a river.

The sweep of the wind; the tangle of leaves; the hush of moving water. The cemetery gives off visions of the grave. Jaundiced children with distended bellies; skeletal old women; drowned and bloated men; blood. Shredded throats, carved breasts. The milk swollen. The promise choked. The scent of remorse.

And she walks past. Past strains of faraway drinking songs echoing between hills. Past the smell of burnt corn, of lamb on the spit, of woodfire. She walks past white-gowned choirboys trickling towards homes; past the ailanthus tree where a girl, hair in cornrows, lies beneath an umbrella; past the noise of someone loving someone else among the azaleas. Past the strained and plaintive cries for more and more—she walks, beneath a thunderhead. Past the light rain come for the peonies once planted by lovers or fathers at the bases of graves. She walks by. Past windbent trees, a barn and silo, smallclothes pinned to a line. Past men with love-bemisted minds, past a grandfather perched on an undersized rocker, humming off-key and knitting stockings for the smallest granddaughter.

We watch the journeywoman walk by, head low, eyes narrow. Listen to the patter of that which drips from the gunnysack. Twilight swarms behind the drum of barefeet. The sun's light fails to blind us to the stars. We watch the walk into darkness. Swollen woman. Womb's contents feel a part. And apart. Twinned heartbeats. Wind in gales—she walks. Trembling aspen leaves; watchfires dotting hills behind the cemetery; gravestones looming in shallow light. Walking past a pit dug for the wicked. The downcast eye. Walk past—*yes*, walk past. Arms cup her belly. Her. She. Journeywoman. Mother. Sundress colored by blue potatoes, knees bruised by falls, feet cut by stones. Legs as longstanding as religion. We, we who know nothing but the watch of the mother, see the shadows converge behind her. See the haze of clouds against the horizon as she walks. As she walks on the dirt road. Walks against the flow of the river. Face lifted. Footsteps. We. We who walk through the valley. Mottled light against leaves under wind. Nightbirds. Her voice may sound like grace. Singing. Come, now. We follow.

Two men find the countryroad woman. Two men. High and Ollie. High and Ollie dirtroading, shooting at crows through truck windows, sharing a half-empty thermos of homebrew.

—*Hey, High, we pass a sweet bitch picking berries?*

—*Pull on over.*

So it happens. Narrow evergreens border the road. Townlights blink distantly. Countryroad woman reaches tall for blackberries, yellow dress slips up on thighs, body tenses and curves as she leans to the brambles. Pickup bounces by, trailing dust, men at the windows. Bored and waiting men. Men who wait for all the things they're sure they should have got but didn't. Here she is. Shoulder-tossed. Bitch-whipped. Limbs pressed against the flatbed. Handsewn dress a yellow rag.

—*What's yer name?*

Countryroad woman mumbles. Crosses bare legs. Closes eyes. Trembles.

—*What it say, Ollie?*

—*Think it say Elly.*

—*Elly ain't yer name no more.*

Cecilia and Grandmother Furne walk toward town. They walk through forest. The path is worn, leaf laden, heavy with light. The sound of footfall resounds between hills. Grandmother Furne wears black woolens. She walks with an oak cane and breathes heavily. With one hand, Cecilia clutches a bead purse. With the other, she holds her Grandmother's dress.

—*Gammy Furne, where mama been?*

—*Well. What age you at?*

—*Nine, Gammy.*

—*You're gettin' on then.*

—*My mama. Where she go?*

—*Ain't for us to know, child.*

They stop beneath the shade of a hornbeam tree. The sun casts long shadows. The air's flavored of strawberries. Shrub fires dot the hills. Cecilia points to the hornbeam.

—*Gammy, that tree's losing its skin.*

—*Seems to be.*

Spreading her skirt neatly beneath her, Grandmother Furne sits beneath the tree. She takes two red pears from her jacket pocket, rubs them against her thigh, passes one to Cecilia. Cecilia pulls her own skirt above one knee to fuss with a scab.

—*Your pear, child. Eat.*

—*Mama dead. Isn't she, Gammy Furne?*

—*Don't speak such things.*

—*I knowed it, she gone.*

—*No telling, child. We wait and see.*

Countryroad woman. Elly. Nylons in ribbons. Mouth stretching into the shape of the sound in whore or howl. Hands reach toward townlight. Across the ground flies the shadow of outstretched wings. What vista is this? Who brings these visions? What else may come?

—*Show 'er yer shit, Ollie.*

—*Hold 'er good.*

—*Make the bitch holler.*

Faint shrill cries. Hurt. Shuddering hips. They take turns lying on top of her.

—*Get off, mutherfucker. Fair's fair.*

—*Hold 'er legs open.*

Two men. High and Ollie. Kick her out of the flatbed. Have at her in the mud. They're out to bury themselves in this woman. To answer all questions of capacity. How much can be borne? The void belongs to whom? Who among us wears the face of the deep?

Faraway bells toll. Bootheels dig against kidneys. Hands are wet by mouth.

—*Flip 'er over, Ollie. Grease 'er with yer finger.*

Countryroad woman. Elly. White skin naked against mud. Low screams. Fainting. Intestinal shuffle and shudder. Hands rake mud; nails break against stone. Mosquitoes circle. Owl calls penetrate the twilight.

She still walks. She. Her. Mother. Jouneywoman singing to the unborn, limping yet lightfoot, stride as remorseless as the seasons. The cold twilight air smells of rain. She walks by us. The sack leaks. Two loaves of bread, the space it takes—the gunnysack. Brown near her hand; black near the curved bottom. Air thickens. The strain of the sack's weight gathers, stretches, releases another drop for the trail that follows. Barefeet treat the earth like a drumhead. Must she walk until the singing fails to cease? We listen. Listen to the haunt of the wind; the birthcry of nightbirds; the swell of the river. Moonlight. Listen as she walks past a chorus of women singing songs to relieve grief. Past the gentle glow of kerosene lamps. Past a shirtless boy, hands full of river agates, wading the edgewater. Past the open-doored chapel, the men in dark coattails, the women in veils. Past the rose wreath, the eulogy, the mourning song.

She walks past the well-lit kitchen. Past the kitchen turned birthing room where the midwife sweats to the muscle heave and uterine clench, to the ghostwalk of communal heartbreak, until, so sudden, the highabove screaming of a voice where once there was none. She walks past the hollow, overwhelming emptiness of division, of one becoming two. Past two held together by the string of the umbilical connection; past the highgloss of steel and loss; and then, in the bittersweet moment of panting and cleaning and whisking away in porcelains of tissue and blood, *sweet Jesus*, the shudderache of separation. The journeywoman walks past. The girlchild. Who does she belong to now? What waters shall bear her? What toward? What ghosts will watch her walk? Can our footsteps lead anywhere but home?

Fingers tear at folds of skin. Sweatslick bodies fumble. The longitude of belief stretches; mouths cut breasts; knuckles loosen teeth. Blood vapor.

The forgotten business of sacks and organs. The piss and shit vales.

—*Bitch ain't pretty no more.*

—*Listen to 'er grunt.*

—*What a tongue on 'er.*

Countryroad woman. Elly. Knee-jerked, bedraggled. Wet-thighed. Time drains away and returns twisted. Colors reduce to mutter, the glide of pain's measure, introduction and reintroduction, space reduced to the ring of emptiness, the sound of a belt unbuckling again. Open-mouthed. Saliva. What will be left behind? Whimpers cease. Tears recede. Legs stiffen. Encroaching visions of the church steeple and stained glass; the lime and granite rectory; translucent women—ageless, long-haired figures of habits and crosses—with light angling through them. The blood rises. Days pass away like smoke. Bones burn like a furnace. The spit and slap of love overridden by choral singing. Hands clamp over bloodied mouth. By the distant townlights, above lime and granite, bells toll. What songs might she sing would her mouth open?

—*Why's she gone quiet, High?*

—*Don't know.*

—*Ain't so good no more.*

—*Let's string 'er up.*

—*String 'er?*

String her by jumper cables and joined wrists from a pine tree. Open her stomach with a hunting knife.

—*Cut the slut's feet.*

Terrorscreams. Highpitched. Endtrailing.

—*Not 'er toes, shitass.*

—*Didn't say that, High.*

—*Go at it again.*

Two men. High and Ollie. Pickup kicking dust behind spinning wheels. Leaving to the song of gunfire. Who will stay behind to mourn?

Here she is. Elly. Countryroad woman left to dangle until bad knots and bloodslick set her loose. Holding her stomach. Drunk on hurt. Spilling organs. Limping toward the river where, around her feet, angelfish will swim.

THE BOY. The dog. The blood. Darkness has come upon him like a stranger. The moon blanches fields of wheat. Indigo sky shows through cloudbreaks. Nightfires. The boy, this Gil, smells the bloodwinds. He cries. He thinks that the fire behind him at home's hearth might warm him; that the stillborn in the compost came in foretelling; that he's been dog-dragged to the valley where the dead belong; that spirits rather than winds cause the wheat to bend and wave. The gazehound drags him forward. The dog eats ground. The boy yaws through the night past the chained men among the poppies singing of the weary years coming to end like a sigh. Past opossums and nightbirds. Past the rounded hill that blocks the view of the horizon and the tree that still burns. Gill sees the wheat sway and fall before spectral feet. He sees the shades among the fields, but he closes his eyes. He doesn't want to see us. What are we but visions come in blessing?

GRANDMOTHER FURNE and Cecilia come near town. The forest gives way to crops. Alfalfa fields lie cut. Grandmother Furne stops to rest often. She sweats.

—*Cecilia, what songs you know?*

—*Just church ones.*

—*Them'll do. Go on now.*

—*You too, Gammy?*

—*My voice ain't here. You're solo.*

The alfalfa flats lie cut. The heavy late-day light casts the fields in orange. Grandmother Furne gasps, shudders, sits in the aftergrass, asks Cecilia if grace might be found in the singing or in the song.

—*Gammy? Gammy, you okay?*

—*Could be I'll sleep a minute. Get on, Cecilia. Sing.*

We. We are the air in the fields of wheat. We are. We are following the journeywoman past a whirlwind of dirt and leaves. Past a tree stump where a knotted seamstress, head handkerchiefed and body aproned, sits with three children on her knees. Past the barrelfire where grangers gather to croon; past the mouthharp, the mandolin, the fiddle; past the middle-C chorus that begins, *She bled and died for me.* Past the unharnessing of oxen; past the mountebank selling glitz and miracle; past families whose more gentle members call out in question—call in voices that are ours: What might be carried in a gunnysack? Why does she clutch at her throat, gag, spit in the road? What words does she sing? A dog howls. She stops, rubs her hands low against her back, gazes on distant systems of light. The low-lying fringe of the blue dress is wet. Did she wade the river? Does she have shoes? Did she cut her feet on sharp riverstones? Has she been crying? Has she been loved? Has she a name?

Here she is. Countryroad woman. Elly. Naked as the new born. She is standing by the river. Gutted. Quiet. Trembling. Skin streaked by blood and spit and semen. Whitewater. Fish swim the shallows; willows line the riverbank; windswept leaves rasp across ground. High above, in an ailanthus tree, a snow owl spreads its wings.

What might be left behind? The puddles of fluids; the furrows left by fingernails; the imprint of a face in the mud.

Whose eyes will spill the summary of a life's grief?

She is standing in the river. Ankles touched by shallows. Angelfish. Bluegill. Bloodclouds mask her feet; the snow owl glides upriver; the angelfish swim. We. We are the dust and stones, and we are the street. We are the roots and reeds, and when angels leap high. Over lilies. We. We see. Watergleam. Translucence. Light behind snow-white wings.

Pucker Up

Into every intelligence there is a door which is never closed.
–Ralph Waldo Emerson

Sometimes all Newell could think about was kissing them on the mouth, these women. He strolled the perimeter of Haish's Agricultural Supply store, following them, listening. He imagined their thoughts: what television shows were on that evening, how to mix cement, their infidelity to their husbands. He followed the tall, colored heels, or the blouses with built-in support, or the tight sandals, or the sundresses that flowed around them like the simple, unimaginative boundaries of their lives.

The security guard, Newell Kind, was bored. It was a boring job. He bent over to adjust the salt blocks on the lower shelves so that he could get a better look at their legs. He followed their smells, like trails of lilac or ocean or crème de menthe, until they stopped to look down at something, at bags of fertilizer or wind chimes or bypass loppers, and the store's artificial light made their skin look so vulnerable and thin, and the whole place smelled of wet earth.

The automatic front doors of Haish's Ag Supply gushed open and the warm, wet air flooded inside. The woman who came in wore an off-white jumper and blue jeans, and she had a pale heart-shaped face, and for a minute Newell mistook her for another woman, a woman he knew named Sester Laura, who he might technically be dating, he wasn't sure. But this wasn't Sester. This woman's limbs were thick and her skin was the color of a potato and she looked too healthy to be into him, but he went up and introduced himself and asked if she needed help finding anything. She wanted to look at artificial ponds and aquatic plants, and as they walked together he talked about himself and asked her questions. Her lips were brightly colored, like pomegranates, and he showed her the heavy-duty polyethylene basins and the waterfall and the flowering water lilies, and her feet moved back and forth like someone slowly running away.

THAT MORNING NEWELL had lain in his bed while someone knocked quietly on the door. He was covered in sweat. He wore only his underpants and he couldn't remember where he'd been the night before. He opened his eyes and placed himself in his own third-floor apartment on Gurler Street. There was a mess of prescription bottles on the floor beside the bed. He only lived temporarily in this shitheap in Rockford, Illinois. Why wasn't there a single thing up on any wall? Why didn't he have a single photo? The furniture—a beaten orange and brown couch, a plywood table scratched with names he didn't know, a woman's vanity filled with someone else's underclothes—had been supplied by Mrs. Muroz, his landlord, who lived on the first floor and who now lightly knocked on the door with one hand, while in the other holding a plastic tray. Underneath the Saran Wrap sat raspberry vol-au-vents and cream puffs and mille feuilles that she'd made by hand. Newell could hear from below him some kind of blurry eastern European music with horns.

Newell got out of bed and opened the thin door and there stood Mrs. Muroz. She was a little heavy-set and getting older. The pastries balanced lightly in her hand. Newell looked past her into the stairwell and cleared his throat. Mrs. Muroz looked wet, as if she'd just been washed. She didn't say a thing but seemed to ask something of him anyway.

SOMETIMES THERE WAS NOTHING to do but watch the front door and wonder what would come next. People came into the store. There were young people and old people, men and women, couples, families. A set of grandparents and three grandchildren came for sand to fill a box. A woman dressed like a prostitute hunted for a toilet seat. A drunk stumbled over a birdbath and lay in an aisle for ten minutes until the other security guard, Rob Patchett, helped him up. A youngish man missing a leg rode in on an electric wheelchair.

Sometimes someone Newell knew came in to the agricultural supply store, like the ex-pastor he'd met a few times at NA meetings. He wore all black but no collar. Newell thought his name was Greg, but he wasn't sure. The ex-pastor walked in with one leg seeming to drag the other forward, as though at least half of him would rather not be moving. The ex-pastor looked around and saw Newell. His face looked like he'd sniffed something unidentifiably off. The ex-pastor walked into Aisle 2 and felt or saw Newell's badge and blue uniform hurrying after him, and his hand clutched at the leg that would rather not move.

Newell said, "Hey!" and his feet shifted back and forth. There was the sound of high heels walking in the next aisle.

"I thought maybe we knew each other," said the ex-pastor. "I'm Greg."

All of a sudden the store was entirely quiet. Nothing moved or stirred and Newell watched Greg's hands slipping into his pockets. He wanted to say something, to have something nice to offer. "You need help?"

"Help with what?"

"Can I help you find something?"

"Carbon filter," Greg said. "Extractor fan. Fertilizer. High-pressure sodium lights."

"Start in Aisle 4."

Greg nodded.

"Over by the gro-lights," Newell said. "You garden?"

"No."

"You have a minute?" Newell asked. "I want to show you something in the back of the store."

He took him by the trash compactor and let him run it once and hear the sound of giant sheets of metal squeezing past one another, and then showed him the truck bays and the stock room and then that was it, that was all there was to see, and Newell requisitioned the emergency Budweiser he'd stashed among hundreds of miles of galvanized electric fence wire. The lights in the stock room were fluorescent and overly bright. So when they burst into the break room, pitch dark and adumbrative, they stood blinking and waiting for their eyes to adjust.

Newell's hands fumbled against the wall until he found the switch and the lights came on. They sat across from one another. They opened cans of beer. Newell told a joke. "Two Scottish nuns are headed for America by boat. The Mother Superior says, 'It's said that the people of this country eat dogs.' 'That's repulsive,' says the second nun. 'Nonetheless,' says the mother superior, 'we shall do as they do.' So just off their boat they find a man selling hot dogs from a cart. They march up and the mother superior orders, 'Two dogs, please.' The man with the cart gives them two hot dogs wrapped in tin foil, and the two nuns sit on a bench beside one another. The younger nun sighs. The mother superior is the first to unwrap her dog. She stares into her tinfoil and blushes a deep red. She leans over to the other nun. She whispers, 'What part did you get?'"

The ex-pastor laughed and pounded on the table. He said, "I needed this." He drank half of his third beer in a single pull. He said, "You know I'm living out of a van?"

Sometimes when Newell couldn't take himself anymore, he headed into the cloying sweet pollen of Lawn & Garden and walked the rows of dirt-filled plastic pots, and sometimes he pressed a finger into a dirt pot and wondered what new thing would grow in all those identical containers, and the irrigation system gave a mechanical chirp, and water began spraying from black hoses and mist hung in the air, and the wet earth smelled fetid and sexualized, like something inside him.

Before noon, Newell took the ex-pastor to the Service Desk and introduced him to Millicent, who had big hair and a harelip but was still sexy. Right away they got into it, touching each other in incidental places like shoulders and elbows. She told him to stop in the way that really means to go on.

Newell left them alone, and went to the bathroom to straighten his uniform, and wandered down Aisle 2 and sat for a minute on a riding lawnmower, and then when he found them again, the ex-pastor had Millicent's shirt pulled halfway up in Aisle 11. Newell wanted them to keep going. He wanted to watch them. He hunkered down, half hiding behind a stack of 17-Gallon Galvanized Wash Tubs. He wanted them to forget where they were, to strip off their clothes and fuck each other in the aisle. But he watched the way the ex-pastor touched her bare side and he knew that they weren't going to. In a moment, they would recover themselves, would retuck their shirts in their pants and wipe their wet mouths. What was left was like a closing window. Just a little sliver of one or two minutes in which the ex-pastor would reach up her shirt. Her skin would feel as hot as a lake of fire. He would press his mouth against her mouth—awkwardly—as if halfway between giving and receiving CPR.

The store owner, Mr. Haish, wasn't coming in, so Newell went into the fenced-in outdoor section of Lawn & Garden to find the other security guard. His name was Rob Patchett, but he went by Patch. Newell walked beneath the green limbs of balled and burlapped trees, and he turned his face up toward the grey clouds that hung from the sky like fat on an upper arm. Patch sat under a medium-sized cypress near the chain-link.

The air was dark and filled with a fine but grainy moisture that felt like wet dust. Newell sat down on the cement as though he were outside in the grass under the sun. "No way," Patch said.

Newell poked at his lower lip. "No way what?"

"No way, I'm clean," said Patch. "I'm telling you, man, I'm a *semi-former* junkie."

"Since when?" The clouds broke into pieces and sunspots polkadotted the ground. "This morning?"

"Since whenever," said Patch. "Who cares?"

"*Semi*-former? Patch, man, you look like shit."

"What do you mean?" Patch peered down at himself over his nose.

"You're filthy."

"So?"

"Look at the color of your uniform."

"Fuck you."

"It's supposed to be blue." Patch didn't say anything. "Come on, man," Newell said, "I need you on this."

They sat for a little while before they got up and locked themselves in the employee bathroom and inhaled starter fluid until the lights were ringed by hundreds of concentric circles and the bathroom began to spin on an unseen axis, and Patch said, "It's puce," and Newell said, "What?" and Patch said, "The color of my uniform is puce." The whole room smelled good, like it might explode, and they shoved each other back and forth between the walls of the toilet stall, and they grappled over the last of the can of starter fluid on the dirty tiles. Things got pretty noisy and one of them put their finger to their lips and shushed, and then somebody, one of the cashiers, started pounding on the door, pounding and pounding hard, as with the heel of her palm, and shouting too, loudly, with words that neither of them could quite make out.

AT LUNCHTIME Newell sat by himself at a table in the break room. He bought a package of pretzels from a vending machine. The lights hummed like jar flies. He thought that he shouldn't believe what his own mind was telling him. He thought of how pretty, harelip Millicent, who worked at the Service Desk, had pounded on the bathroom door and then written both him and Patch up. He pushed his pretzels away and laid his head on his arms. He tried to think about how the overhead lights worked, and he thought something about argon gas, and glass tubes, and electricity, and then he couldn't get anywhere; and his thigh muscles jumped and he tried to think about how his musculature worked, and he thought of tendons in the shape of anchors, of myofibrils and contractile tissue, and then he couldn't get any further. His forehead touched the cool table beneath him; he believed it was cold. He believed in his thighs and his arms. He believed in the smell of old cigarettes, and warning notices, and humming lights, and burnt coffee, and mildew.

WHEN SHE CAME IN looking for him, he sat in the back office watching her breasts on the security cameras. It was Sester Laura. Whenever he thought about her, his skin began to burn. He touched the screen. She had on a thin pale dress with thin dark straps, and her skin was whiter than paper. She looked like a sexy dead thing. She talked to Millicent at Customer Service, and on the monitor Newell watched their lips move without sound. Then Millicent picked up the phone. Above him a loud-speaker cracked and Millicent spoke into the phone and the loudspeaker said, "NEWELL TO CUSTOMER SERVICE PLEASE. NEWELL TO CUSTOMER SERVICE."

When he met Sester Laura at the Service Desk, he said, "Didn't know when I'd see you."

"Right now."

Newell touched her on the back of the arm, cautiously, the way he might reach out to touch a fence to test if it was electrified. Then he led her outside into Lawn & Garden. It was near sunset. Hundreds of orchids spindled up from pots. He leaned in so that his lips were close to her ear. He said, "I've been watching other women all day long."

"Great," she said.

"I'm getting sick of myself," he said.

"I'm sick of you, too."

They sat on large overturned planters and Newell watched Sester Laura's fingers twitch. He said, "You want to make out?"

"Not really."

"I've got some pills."

"What sort?"

"I'm not sure. A mix."

"Let me see." She held out her hand. He passed her a medicine vial and she flicked through the pills on her palm. She held up two, and she said, "Darvon?" and they both took one and then they wandered around laughing.

He pushed her along the aisles in the tray of a red AMES two-wheeled wheelbarrow.

He showed her the round sandstone stepping stones and, holding on to one another, they both stood on a single stone.

She chased him up and down the aisles with a double bit axe. Newell breathed hard. He stopped to rest his hands on his knees in front of a barbecue grill. In the stainless steel reflection of its hood, a blurred Sester Laura leaned forward and rested her head against Newell's back, and they stood like that, folded together, until they heard a loud whistle and then, from the front of the store, a scream.

AFTERWARD, THE SUN balanced on the iron wire of the horizon. Newell and Sester Laura walked into the parking lot. They had blood on their knees and their hands. In the middle of the lot, Newell saw an old blue van. The ex-pastor stuck his hand out a window of the van and waved. They walked toward him. His hand was up and it was as if he was reaching up into the sun.

The ex-pastor pulled two beers from the front seat and held them out toward them and said, "You kill somebody?"

Nobody answered and they sat in the orange light and the quiet and they drank. A woman in a salmon-colored blazer walked past with short quick steps toward her car, her heels tapping against the cement like the second hand of a clock, and she looked at the blue van in the orange light and saw the shadows of three people inside.

"Okay," the ex-pastor said, "I won't ask again." He gestured loosely at the blood on their clothes with the back of his hand.

A TALL MAN had lain on the floor just inside the door and bled and screamed. "It's in my thigh," he screamed. "Take it out!" His breath came in small gusts. A triangular piece of silvery metal jutted from his leg.

Newell and Sester Laura had slipped behind the Service Desk where Millicent stood wailing like a dog. "A car," the man gasped. "Hit by a car." He stood and began to drag himself over to the Service Desk. Blood flowed out of his leg and across the floor in quick little rivers.

Behind the Service Desk, Millicent stammered, and a crowd of customers gathered. Some people made little sounds like *ahhhh* or *ohhhh*. Others headed for the door.

"Take it out!" the tall man screamed.

Millicent grabbed Newell by the arm. "What do we do?"

"Call somebody?" Newell said. He thought about the particular blood patterns on the floor, and about how one decided what to do in a situation like this.

"An ambulance!" said Sester.

The tall man reached down and grabbed the silvery metal sticking in his thigh and pulled and blood fountained over his hand. The metal didn't budge. "Get it out! Get it out!" He lay down on the floor in front of the

Service Desk. Millicent took up the phone and began to dial. Newell registered that people were looking at his uniform with vague expectation, and he pushed aside two little boys, pulling Sester Laura with him, and they knelt by the wounded man.

Sester took the tall man's hand. His eyes rolled like marbles in his head. She said, "God, you're fucked up." He was kind of nice looking. Very tall. A slightly off-center nose and brown eyes and a cleft chin.

His right hand clutched opened and closed, opened and closed against the cement floor. "The car," he said. "I couldn't see it." He screamed. He said, "Get the fucking thing out!"

Newell pulled off his belt. He looped it around the man's thigh, pushed it up toward his groin and tightened it. He touched the man on the shoulder. He said, "Hey, what's your name?" and then he grabbed the metal and pulled.

The tall man screamed. Blood arced once, then again. Newell felt something pulling back against him as if he was in a kind of tug-of-war, and then it came out in his hands. He looked at it. A silver hunk of metal. Threads of flesh. There was a smell, too, like either a menstruating woman or the ocean.

The tourniqueted leg began to turn white. The man's eyes were closed but his lips were moving. He whispered something that neither Newell nor Sester could hear. Someone said, "What's he saying?" but they could only hear the approaching siren of the ambulance. His skin was so pale. His lips moved again, and they leaned forward. They were in a huge puddle of blood. They leaned in closer so that his lips almost touched their ears.

A DARK ORANGE LIGHT slanted in the window of the ex-pastor's van. In the back of the van there was a bed wide enough for the three of them to sit on. Near the front of the store, an ambulance flashed its lights in the loading zone. Sester Laura's skin seemed to absorb the light, to soak it up like a sponge.

"You live in this van?" Newell said. He turned his head toward the ex-pastor.

"Yeah," said the ex-pastor. He had an Oldstyle halfway to his mouth.

"What happened?"

"What do you mean what happened?"

"You get kicked out of your old place or something?"

"Nothing happened."

"There had to be something."

"Nothing I could see. It all was too slow to observe."

Newell's apartment smelled like insecticide. Headlights broke against the windows and flashed against the walls like an ambulance's lights. They were beside one another on a mattress. It was a twin so they were necessarily close. They were fully clothed under a threadbare blanket. They touched each other without urgency, as if they were bored. They held their lips together.

There was an empty pill bottle beside the mattress, and a hair dryer, and a tube of personal lubricant, and two glasses of water. They could hear someone crying below them. A long series of staggered cries. Then a high-pitched stuttering. Then a bit of quiet before it all started again.

After a while of this, Sester Laura pushed up on her elbows. "What the fuck's wrong with this place?"

"It's the landlady."

"Is she always making so much noise?"

"I don't think so." The moonlight cut in the window and cast a white rectangular shape at the foot of the bed. Sester Laura's neck bent down as though she were looking through the mattress and the floorboards and into the bathroom where a heavy-set, aging woman curled around the base of a pink toilet.

"What's her name?" she said.

"Mrs. Muroz."

They lay in the bed, unable. Mrs. Muroz wailed below them. Sester Laura covered her head with a pillow. Between the buttons of her shirt,

Newell could see that her bra was the color of congealed blood. After awhile, he stood up. He said, "Maybe we ought to go down there?" and he took Sester's hand and helped her out of the bed, and they walked out of the apartment together and down the stairs. They knocked at the door and, while they waited, Sester leaned in toward his ear. But then they heard the thump of feet walking toward them. The door opened inward, a growing line of light, and Mrs. Muroz stood there wearing a tight aquamarine housedress. Her swollen eyes looked up at them.

"I am sorry," she said. She sniffled. "I cannot help the noise."

"It's not the noise," Sester Laura said. "We wanted to see if everything's okay."

"No." She stood there looking at them, holding her own shoulders.

"No?" Sester Laura said, "Should we call somebody?"

"Who?" said Mrs. Muroz.

No one could think of what to do or say next. They stood in silence with the open door between them. Mrs. Muroz was crying quietly. She looked at them, their sad faces, and she thought that maybe she would invite them in.

The Hospital

A T THE HOSPITAL I found this duffel bag in my hands, and in the
duffel bag my wife's sateen nightclothes and blue jeans and a blouse
and two pairs of white sport socks and two pairs of panties and her con-
tacts and saline solution and eye glasses and a yellow legal pad and a blue
pen. A huddle of white-coated doctors near the bed mumbled things
like *brain stem* and *medulla oblongata* and *ischemic cascade* and *hemorrhagic
damage*. They used a blue-tubed ventilator to make my wife breathe. I
asked, Does Maddy have to be made to breathe? She can't breathe on her
own? The head whitecoat's name was Espiritu and he dealt with brains
and had a face like an aging mushroom. He looked startled. He said, Oh
no not on her own.

I asked a kind-faced nurse, Do you know what's wrong with her?
and she said, Strokes, and she said, More than one, and I said, How
many more than one? and she said, Five. I said, What's your name? and
she said, My name is Nurse Kishwater.

At the hospital, in those first hours, I'd done what anyone would
do. Anyone would have sat with her all night, and held her hand, and
walked beside her when she was transferred from the ER to the I.C.U.
The walls were white, and the sky outside the window white, and Maddy's face white. The bed could be controlled by a remote that canti-

levered Maddy's torso toward me or away. All night the wall-mounted television spoke of explosions and flashed images of blurry foreign faces captured on closed-circuit TVs. When morning came, I picked up the beige phone corded to the wall. I dialed and Maddy's mother answered, and I said, Evelyn? and she said, Yes, and I said, It's Thom.

Evelyn said, What's wrong? and I said, Maddy's in the hospital, and Evelyn said, What hospital? and I said, She can't move, and she said, Is she going to be alright? and I said, I don't know, and she said, What about the baby?

Static played on the line. There was a sound like a hiccup. Down the hall I could hear someone cough. Evelyn asked, What do the doctors say? and I said, They don't know, and she asked, What about her work? and I said, What about it? and she said, Is she still teaching? and I said, She's in the hospital Evelyn, and I said, She can't move, and she said, Should we come? and I said, I think so.

The silence on the line stretched out until in its length and breadth I felt the miles and miles of road between Chicago and Las Vegas. Evelyn's breathing fluttered over the wires. I said, Tell Dick that you should probably come.

THIS IS A SAD STORY, and it's a long story, and it's yours as much as it is mine, and it's a hospital story, too.

IN THE I.C.U., I pulled the green chair closer to Maddy's bed. The rise of her chest came along with the wheeze of the ventilator. A blue tube ran into her mouth. Muscles jerked in the right side of her face. I sat and I sat, and when I began to talk, I couldn't stop. I went on about the details of porch building and architectural salvage, and rehashed a conversation we'd had about coffee beans and percolators, and about the pros and cons of ash verses oak, and described the hospital room's contents (the ventilator, the tulips, the blue blanket across her legs). I talked a long time on the predicted mildness of the oncoming winter. Two hours of uninterrupted one-sided talking before the edges of things blurred. The armchair beneath me sagged. My voice graveled and my throat ached. Maddy seemed to sleep, but *sleep* wasn't the right word. The thin yellow light canting in the window caught against bits of polished steel. I flicked on the TV. Explosions lit the night sky. Airplanes seeded clouds with silver iodide and dry ice. A pale blue house floated down the Mississippi river. A line of corpses in mud. Reeds bending in half beneath wind. A decapitated head.

THE HUMAN BODY is a cruel miracle. Housed inside it—the whitish flake of skin, and the dried blood of lips, and the crack and peel, and the fall of hair, and the held or absent breath—is a story that can't be told. It is a story that just *happens*.

THE NEUROLOGIST, Dr. Espiritu, led me into the hall to discuss Maddy's condition. Whitish early afternoon light seeped in the windows. The sun looked like a pupil. I hadn't slept in three days. Dr. Espiritu's white coat was pockmarked with light brown stains and it hitched up and down as he spoke in a hushed voice. He was a strangely gray and ill-defined man. Like a fungus.

He said, Madeleine is semi-vegetative. He said, An MRI gives us pictures of Madeleine's brain. He used words like *stem* and *pons* and *cerebellum*. He said, She can think but she can't move. I said, The brain has a stem? and I said, Like a flower? and he said, The brainstem is the seat of consciousness, and I repeated, The brainstem is the seat, and he said, Your wife moves in and out of consciousness because the brainstem has been irreparably damaged.

The prognosis was, and I quote exactly, *Not good, not good at all.*

Nurse Kishwater walked past with her shoes tapping briskly and gave a small wave. The air smelled like rain. Dr. Espiritu wanted to speak of how we might limit future life-saving measures.

I said, Will she open her eyes? and he said, I don't know.

I said, Does she remember everything? and he said, She remembers.

I said, Have you ever known anyone in a similar condition who's improved? and he said, Yes, and I said, That's good, and he said, This is the most unlikely outcome. He looked at his watch twice, and I understood he had others to look after. I thanked him. I told him no—I wasn't ready to make this decision. Despite his flaccid gray face, his eyes were those of a kind man.

I said, She knows who I am? and he said, She knows who you are.

The nurses' footsteps clacked in nearby rooms and a child cried and there was deep even breathing and a steady *click click click* and a feathery whoosh and an erratic beep.

I said, What about the baby? and Dr. Espiritu said, Currently he's fine, and I said, It's a boy? and he said blinked twice before he said, You didn't know? and he said, The ultrasound technician was 95% sure, and I said, A boy! and he said, Mr. Poole, and I said, Yes? and he said, I need you to understand that before twenty-four weeks there is little chance of survival, and I said, Maddy's twenty-two weeks, and Doctor Espiritu said, After twenty-four weeks we could consider a C-section, and I said, Maddy's twenty-two weeks, and he said, I know.

A HOSPITAL REQUIRES INJURY and illness and disease. A hospital does not seek to prevent harm but to heal it. It is a house for the broken and the sick. The story of the hospital is the story of a kind man who splints the leg of a beaten child. But the story of the hospital is also the story of a kind man who leaves the child when his shift is over. The kind man has his own kind children.

THE PHONE RANG, and for a while I stared at it rather than answering. It chirruped like an insect. When I picked up the receiver it was cold against my cheek, and I held it there, and I didn't speak. A woman's voice said,

Hello?

Then the voice said, It's Evelyn.

Then Evelyn said, Are you there Thom?

The lights around me were ringed with concentric circles. Evelyn said, I can hear you breathing, and I said, She hasn't gotten better Evelyn, and she said, Dick called the hospital, and she said, Madeleine's only thirty years old, and she said, Dick says she's too young to have a stroke.

Horns blew in from the street.

Evelyn said, Dick wants to know what you have been doing that Maddy had a stroke, and I said, Jesus Christ. She said, Dick says this might be some lifestyle thing, and I said, Put Dick on the phone, and she said, Hold on.

I heard the soft rubbing sound of Evelyn's hands covering the phone and then muffled voices, and then Evelyn took a deep breath that blew across the line. She said, He doesn't want to talk to you, and I said, This wasn't our fault Evelyn, and she said, We've got tickets, and I said, Did you hear me Evelyn? and she said, We're flying in on Thursday, and I said, We didn't do anything. The line went dead and I rose and stumbled out of the room and down the hall and into the empty waiting room. The room felt dizzy and the pictures on the wall were of indiscriminate seashores and I moved in circles and I quietly said, Crap. My right hand slapped the wall, but the wall was unblemished and my hand hurt, and I said, Shit! loudly, and then I yelled worse things until Nurse Kishwater hurried toward me. She said, Mr. Poole, and I said, Yes, and I was breathing hard and she said, I get that you're pissed off. Her eyes weren't pinched in anger but open, and I hit the wall again until pain sealed my hand into a fist and the nurse whispered, Quietly Mr. Poole, and she whispered, There's a child just down the hall.

You CAN TELL a hospital story is true if it leaves you with the desire to both turn toward it and away. You can tell it's true when you're stuck between two gestures. Between water flowing into a glass and water flowing out.

Between hello and goodbye.

Early in the morning, two orderlies haunted the I.C.U. The first had skin the color of pitch. With a broom cast over his shoulder, he passed Rm. 413, and stopped in our doorway, and smiled in. The first orderly had close cropped hair, and broad cheeks. He said, Morning, and he tipped his head in the way that men sometimes say hello. His eyes passed over Maddy, and he tipped his head again. He had a kind walrus face with teeth as uneven as old headstones.

After the first orderly came the second. This orderly pushed a bucket with the handle of his mop. Light shone against the white floor. He made a lot of noise, and a wheel of the mop bucket squeaked, and at each step he quivered cutely in the way of an ugly puppy. He did not stop by our doorway. He did not look in. His right eye squinted suspiciously and stayed half closed as though weighted down by his heavy brow.

I'd like to tell you that we're more than the sum of our deformities and strokes and heart attacks and cancers. Even if we're not.

Dick and Evelyn Cavanaugh appeared in the long hospital corridor. Framed by the small rectangular end of the hall they looked like figurines in pantsuits. They held onto one another and shuffled forward as though neither could stand without the support of the other. The automatic doors to the I.C.U. slowly opened. Evelyn touched the tail of her red scarf to her mouth. Dick Cavanaugh was clean-shaven, wore his hair in a flattop, and had lost a share of his extra weight. Both of their faces were composed like puzzle pieces forced into positions in which they did not belong.

When I stood beside them in the hall, Evelyn said, How is she? and I said, She's semi-vegetative, and she said, What's that mean? and then I said, It's hard to say. Dick avoided looking in my direction. Evelyn said, Will she know we're here? and I said, We'd better go see her, and I said, I'm not sure.

In Rm. 413, a white sheet stretched from Maddy's feet to just above her breasts. I said, Your parents are here. We sat in chairs for awhile. Dick Cavanaugh kept getting up out of his chair and looking at the door, and the bright fluorescence of the hall, and the flush of white-shoed nurses, and the chattering of people saying meaningless things in passing to other people, and the clatter of things hitting against other things.

Evelyn kept looking at Maddy and then down at her own shoes. Maddy's dark hair looked freshly washed. Evelyn said, I think you'll be back up to speed in no time, and Dick touched Maddy's arm and said, I can't really think of what I'm supposed to say, and Evelyn said, This is a nice hospital room.

Later, Dick Cavanaugh paced, and he folded a newspaper over his protruding belly and barely glanced at his daughter. He said, Goddamnit. He straightened Maddy's sheets. He said, What's that damn thing on her legs? I didn't know the name for the device that cradled her legs and massaged them to protect against her blood clotting. Evelyn Cavanaugh stood in a corner of the room running her scarf through her hands. The hard purple bit of plastic molded to Maddy's finger monitored her heart rate. Dick Cavanaugh said, What's that on her finger? and I said, A pulse oximeter. He navigated the machinery. He said, What's the blue tube in her throat? and I said, It's part of the ventilator. Dick Cavanaugh sat down in the green chair beside the bed. He said, What's the tube in her nose, and I said, That's the feeding tube.

Later still, Dick turned toward Maddy and said, Your mom says you might hear us, and he said, I don't know, and he said, You shouldn't have done this to yourself, and I said, Listen, and I said, She didn't do a goddamn thing, and I said, Maybe you should have talked to her a little more, and he said, She's hard to talk to, and I said, That's your excuse Dick? and I said, Everybody's hard to talk to, and he said, I'm holding you responsible for this, and I said, Fuck you.

Here's a hospital story.

Late one night, you wake up and leave the room to walk the halls. The Orderly of the Crooked Teeth and the Orderly of the Fisheye wheel a man in a bed through the hall. They both wear white. They make almost no noise. The man lies under a blue blanket. His eyes are closed. The skin that can be seen—the face such as it is, and the arms poking from the gown— have dripped and run and sloughed. Like a melted candle.

The Cavanaughs left for their hotel. I sat in the chair reading magazines. I drifted asleep in the chair and woke with a numb leg. But at the foot of the bed, I saw movement beneath the blue blanket. Lifting the covers I said, What was that? Her right big toe moved. It bent down and went rigid as though pointing. I said, You can move your toe! It wiggled again, and I touched the down on her arms. I said, This is good Maddy.

Her eyes opened. Her eyes focused on my face and then on her own toe. She kept blinking like someone trying to clear her blurred vision.

I said, This is very good.

Then I pushed the nurse's call button.

Nurse Kishwater's scrubs had a pink stain in the shape of a carrot. She said, What is it Thom? and I said, She can move her toe, and she said, She can? and I said, Her eyes are open, and she said, They are? and she looked at Maddy and said, They are!

Maddy's eyes moved between Nurse Kishwater and me. Nurse Kishwater said, Well look at that, and I said, Wiggle your toe Maddy! and Maddy's right toe moved back and forth. I said, Do it again Maddy, and she did it again.

Nurse Kishwater said, I've been here thirty-six hours. She said, This is the best thing I've seen in the last two days. She tucked a length of her hair behind an ear and her contact lenses swam in her eyes. She repositioned Maddy's arms and then straightened the pillow beneath her head. Before she left the room she said, It's so nice to see you awake today Madeleine.

When Nurse Kishwater left, I said, Maddy can you blink one long blink for *yes*?

Madeline closed both her eyes long enough that I feared she'd dropped to sleep. Then she opened them wide and looked back. I said, Maddy can you blink two quick blinks for *no*? She gave two blinks—not too rapidly but not so slow as the long *yes* blink. I said, It doesn't matter if you aren't up to it. I said, Ready to try? She blinked once for *yes*. I picked up her hand.

I asked, Are you cold?

Maddy answered, *No.*

Hot?

No.

Can you feel the baby kicking?

Yes.

Are you in any pain?

No.

The baby is a boy, Maddy.

Yes. Yes.

I asked, Don't your lips hurt? and she blinked three times. I asked, What do three blinks mean? No yes?

Yes.

A PROPER HOSPITAL is never empty. The doctors and nurses do not rush but move with quick economical grace. The doctors spend more time with their charts than with their patients. The nurses comfort a stream of patients and families during their long shifts. They have so little time.

IN THE MORNING Evelyn came into Rm. 413, and sat beside Maddy and me, and crossed her legs. The low whoosh of air in the ventilator sounded like water continually running in a toilet. I'd been reading aloud. I said, She's woken up, and then I said, While you were gone she woke up and opened her eyes and moved her toe. And Evelyn said, Her toe? and I said, Yes, and she said, That really good, right? and I said, I think so, and Evelyn said, I want to see her awake too. We sat quietly for a few minutes before Evelyn's lips pursed. She said, Dick thinks you're to blame for this, and I said, I know, and she said, I don't think you are. Then she opened a magazine about country living.

When Dick showed up outside the room, he held a coffee in each of his hands. He gestured to Evelyn through the window, and she put her magazine down, and opened the door to the room and went outside with him. They leaned close to one another. They both wore blue. Their lips moved minimally as if they were whispering to each other. A minute later Evelyn returned. She didn't sit down. She said, Dick wants to come into the room, and I said, Tell him to come in, and she said, He wants me to tell you that he doesn't want you in it. I looked at Maddy and tried to keep quiet. My throat tensed up. Someone down the hallway could not stop coughing. After awhile Evelyn sat back down. She said, I'm sorry. We opened our books and magazines, and we sat that way for a half an hour. Then the hinges squeaked and Dick pushed the door open. He didn't look at me, but he went to stand by Evelyn. His fingers held her shoulder. She put her hand over his. I said, Oh for Christ's sake, and I said, I'm going to the bathroom, and I got up and left.

But in the hall I looked back through the window into Rm. 413 as Dick Cavanaugh sat down in the chair I'd just left. Maddy was beneath a blue blanket. Dick held three fingers of her left hand. Her eyes were closed and her mouth hung open. In the chair Dick's body curled like the letter C. He wore a canvas coat. His jaw moved as though he was speaking, but I couldn't hear any words. I watched Maddy's eyes open and fasten onto him. After a minute, Dick pulled a *Time* magazine from his back pocket.

He opened to a marked page and his mouth began to move. Slowly at first but then faster and faster. Then he rubbed his arms briskly with his hands. A nurse entered the room to record Maddy's vitals, and Dick's thumbs worried the bottom hem of his coat. When the heart monitor began to chirp in alarm, Dick came to his feet. When it stopped he sat down again. His face had flushed red. His eyes had widened. His hands held his chest.

A HOSPITAL STORY is never about the hospital. It's about the scream of a child at night, and about two nurses laughing over a joke about a fat arm and a needle as long as a pencil, and about quiet patients confined to their beds, and about lights bordering darkened windows, and about the coughing that goes on so long down the corridor that like the orderlies you begin wishing that the poor cougher would just die already, and about the hollow whispered prayers at night, and about clasped hands and about finding peace and about the cessation of pain.

AT THE NURSES' DESK Nurse Kishwater asked, What in the world do you want a flashlight for? and I said, We want to shine light on Maddy's abdomen, and she said, That's an idea. Through the windows of the doors to the I.C.U., I saw the Orderly of the Fisheye pushing a boy with cancer in a wheelchair. Nurse Kishwater searched through her desk and loaned me a penlight.

Maddy and I spent the rest of the night ignoring the low voices at the nurses' desk and the string of nurse heads peeking in to see us imagining our baby's movements as we held the light against Maddy's stomach.

With my thumb I moved the lever on the barrel to OFF.

I asked, Is there anything else I can do?

No.

Do you want to sleep, Maddy?

Yes.

Are you too warm?

No.

Too cold?

No.

Do you need anything that I'm not thinking to ask?

No.

Do you feel sad, Maddy?

Yes.

Do you wish, Maddy?

Yes.

Do you think the baby can see the light?

THE STORY OF THE HOSPITAL cannot teach us how to heal ourselves. Nor does it suggest that our ideal condition encompasses neither injury nor sickness. Nor does it suggest that what you love can end in any way but loss.

THE HOSPITAL SMELLED of alcohol and whiffs of bodily function. Nurse Kishwater stood in the doorway of Rm. 413. She said, She's scheduled for another MRI early next week, and I said, Okay, and she said, I've got something you're gonna want to hear, and I said, Maddy's getting better? and she said, Nothing that good. Nurse Kishwater wore no make-up. Her hair had been swept into a bun. She moved with a studied efficiency as she positioned Maddy's arms and legs and then felt Maddy's belly with both palms.

Nurse Kishwater left the room and came back with a bulbous microphone. She cupped it in her palm. I said, What's that? and she said, A Doppler machine. She said, With it we might be able to hear the baby.

Maddy slept. I said, Maddy! and I said, Maddy wake up! Her eyes looked up at me. Her hair curled around her head like a nest. Nurse Kishwater pulled Maddy's shirt above her stomach and covered her stomach with a greenish gel. Then she put the dark microphone to Maddy's belly.

Nurse Kishwater said, She's thin. She said, Things are easier when they're thin. I said, You think she's too thin? and she said, No she's good. She said, Be quiet now.

The heartbeat was a reedy thump-*thump*. One of my hands felt the bones of Maddy's shoulder and the side of her stomach and the underside of her leg and her toe. Thump-*thump*. Nurse Kishwater said, 160 beats per minute, and I said, Is that normal? and she said, It's very good. On the screen Maddy's heartbeat had risen from 62 beats per minute to 95. I said, Hear that Maddy? Her eyes were closed but her toe moved once against my hand.

Here's another hospital story.

The Orderly of the Uneven Teeth stops the Orderly of the Fisheye. They stand close to one another like good friends. The Orderly of the Fisheye has been pushing a cart holding a Styrofoam box. The Orderly of the Uneven Teeth says, What in that box? and the Orderly of the Fisheye says, Nothing no more, and the Orderly of the Uneven Teeth says, What was? and the Orderly of the Fisheye says, Heart.

The moon hung outside the window. Maddy and I were both awake. It was late. Air blowing through the hospital vents sounded like dozens of people murmuring.

I said, Maddy, I need to ask you some things.

She blinked, *Yes*.

I said, Are your parents in the room too much?

No.

I'm trying to get along with them.

Yes.

You want me to get along with them?

Yes.

Do you have any idea how confused I am?

Yes.

Do you hurt?

Yes. No.

Does that mean sometimes?

Yes.

Is there anything I can do now?

No.

Do you feel our son move in the evening?

No.

In the mornings?

Yes.

I'm tired Maddy, are you?

Yes.

I want our normal life.

Yes.

I wish we could sleep together.

Yes.

I don't want to raise this baby alone.

No.

EVERY HOSPITAL STORY is hollow inside. There's no one there, no one *here*, but you.

ON MADDY'S SIXTEENTH DAY at the hospital, I went home to shower, and to change, and to feed the cat. I was in the kitchen when the phone rang. On the far end of the line was Nurse Kishwater. She spoke fast. She used terms like *anticoagulant* and *computed tomography* and *enlarging infarct.* She took pauses and deep breaths. Her dry mouth made small accidental clicking sounds that transmitted across the line.

I jotted all the words down on the note pad on the wall next to the phone. *Reticular formation. Hemorrhagic. Coumadin. Magnetic resonance. Retro-perennial.* The first page of the pad still held a note from Maddy.

154

Thom,

Gone to the store. Maybe artichokes. You love artichokes. I hope you are here when I get back.

Love,

M

Into the phone I said, Nurse Kishwater I don't know what *retro-perennial* means, and she said, Retro*peritoneal*, and I said, I still don't know what it means, and she said, Your wife is bleeding behind the kidneys.

I said, There's a word that means *behind the kidneys*? and Nurse Kishwater said, Dr. Espiritu has taken her off the blood thinner, and I said, Doesn't she need it for the strokes? and she said, We need to stop the bleeding, and she said, That's our priority, and I said, Is she dying? and she said, I don't know, and I said, How is she right now? and she said, Not good, and she said, Still conscious.

A story is an abbreviated truth. There is always more to tell. What little you know of yourself is just the sawdust from a better project.

I called the Cavanaughs at their hotel. I said, I can't say what I need to say, and Dick Cavanaugh said, I've had some experience with that problem. I said, Maddy's stroke is worsening.

There was a problem with the way I was breathing. Dick said, We just left, and I said, I know, and Dick said, We just got back to the hotel, and Dick said, What do the doctors plan to do? and I said, I think she's dying.

Dick said, Oh damn oh damn, and he said, I can't tell Evelyn this. Then he said, Will you talk to her?

I could hear the phone being transferred. A scratch of the receiver against fabric and a knock and a catch of breath and a clearing of throat. Evelyn said,

Dick doesn't look good, and I said, No, and she said, I don't think he can handle this, and I said, I understand, and she said, Tell me what's happened.

This is a story that can't be told because a voice always gives rather than takes away.

Maddy, do you remember the time I made a fort in the living room?
Yes.
Out of the couch and the entertainment center and a bunch of tape?
Yes.
You remember?
Yes.
Remember how mad you were?
No.
You said the tape would leave marks on the furniture.
Yes.
Did it?
Yes.
Remember how we took off our clothes?
Yes.
I love you, Maddy.
Yes.
I can't do this without you.
No.
Do you have things you want to say?
Yes.
Am I asking the right questions?
Yes. No.
Are you frustrated?
Yes.
Can I help?

No.

Oh, God, I want to help.

No.

Are you okay?

No. No.

I HAVE ONE MORE STORY to tell. It is a story about the alarm of the heart monitor. It is a story about fear and sadness and loss, but grief is wordless, and it can't be understood until you've lived with it. And once you've lived with it, you live with it forever.

It is a story about me startling awake and rising.

I'D SLEPT IN THE GREEN ARMCHAIR. The heart monitor chirped like an oversized cricket. The beats per minute slowed. Twenty. Then seven. Then zero.

I tried to say, MADDY? but this was not speech.

Before the flurry of activity and before the doctors and the nurses rushed and before the numbers and Latin phrases and before the wheeled bed moved to an operating room and before someone mentioned *fetal extraction,* there was a long still moment. Sunlight broke against wet glass. Fog swirled around a protean sun. Maddy's dark hair pooled like unspooled thread around her face and shoulders. She lay on her back. Both her arms were at her sides. Her face was a thousand lights being extinguished one after the next.

Dick Cavanaugh stood in the doorway with two paper cups of water spilled at his feet and his hands open and his arms gesturing as scrubs and whitecoats pushed around him. The room swelled like a singing throat. Voices passed from one mouth to the next and someone muttered beneath their breath and a pigeon-chested doctor used the name Epinephrine in vain. The beige-tile floor rose up and lowered me gently to the ground, and the Orderly of the Fisheye and the Orderly of the Uneven Teeth stood me back up. Their breath smelled like coffee and wintergreen. Their arms encircled mine.

I said, CAN YOU TELL ME WHAT'S HAPPENING? and the Orderly of the Uneven Teeth said, You need to sit down Mr. Poole.

Maddy's limbs had disappeared behind a huddle of whitecoats and scrubs. On the gurney her disembodied head lolled from side to side as if she were being shaken. Dust and hair hung in the air and shone against the light.

The Orderly of the Uneven Teeth said, Is he trying to say something? and the Orderly of the Fisheye said, Mr. Poole, you need to speak a little bit louder.

I said, WHERE WILL THEY TAKE HER?

The Orderly of the Uneven Teeth looked at me in the way that a child looks at a sea urchin in a tank. His grip about my arm tightened.

I said, SHE'S NOT DEAD.

The Orderly of the Uneven Teeth said, Mr. Poole we can't hear you.

The Orderly of the Fisheye said, We got to sit you down Mr. Poole.

The Orderly of the Uneven Teeth said, You got to breathe.

Hospital beds have wheels. In a waiting area outside the operating room, Dr. Espiritu shook my shoulders. The Orderly of the Uneven Teeth and the Orderly of the Fisheye placed me in a chair and sat beside me. Dr. Espiritu said, Can you hear me Thom? and I said, OF COURSE I CAN HEAR YOU.

He said, We can't understand you.

He said, Can you speak a little louder?

The air sat and waited like a man about to be hung. My mind fed on pictures of disasters. The sack of cities and blood in streets and burned skin and organs in Styrofoam boxes and bloody lips and piles of bodies and severed heads.

Dr. Espiritu said, Your wife has died. He said, We're taking the baby out through the abdomen.

Dr. Espiritu held my shoulders. His chest touched my arm. His lips moved.

In the operatory, the blood was still warm on the floor. Doctors and nurses wore plastic gloves. A light like a sun shone too bright. They wore aqua-colored aprons and facemasks and rounded hats. Someone less than visible said, *Oh dearohdear.* Maddy was a shape beneath a yellow cloth and an overwhelming sense of how the cloth on the table was not moving.

Beyond the table and the cloth over my wife, a doctor with red fleshy cheeks held the child. The child opened its mouth. It opened its mouth wide and its lips shivered. Its arms raised and it wailed and the doctors and nurses stood around in a semi-circle. My legs walked me past the tables and a porcelain sink and a box of plastic gloves and a scalpel and a defibrillator and airway intubation devices and a resuscitation bag and an incubator and her bare feet beneath the yellow cloth.

I said to Maddy, THIS IS OUR CHILD.

Then, as I stepped past, I touched the yellow cloth and the table and the limbs beneath.

The beige walls of the operating room flexed and pulsed like an artificial heart.

For such a short time, beneath the orange incubator light, you become my story. You move and stretch like warm wax. Your translucent skin is loose. Your eyelids as thin as paper. Your chin quivers. Your eyes are open momentarily. Then they are closed. Then open. Then closed.

The doctor with wide red cheeks appears in front of me in the way that dreams steal on us always unobserved at night. His reddish waxy lips move but there is no sound.

He picks you up and holds you gently for such a large man.

He puts you in my hands.

Just like this.

Silas Dent Zobal was born in Bellingham, Washington, and spent his teenage years in Rockford, Illinois. His fiction has appeared in the *Missouri Review, Glimmer Train, Shenandoah, North American Review,* and many others journals. Stories from *The Inconvenience of the Wings* won the inaugural Discovered Voices Award from the *Iron Horse Literary Review,* a scholarship to the Bread Loaf Writers' Conference, and first place in the *Glimmer Train* Fiction Open. His debut novel, *People of the Broken Neck,* will be released by Unbridled Books in Fall 2016.

Fomite

A fomite is a medium capable of transmitting infectious organisms from one individual to another.

"The activity of art is based on the capacity of people to be infected by the feelings of others." Tolstoy, *What Is Art?*

Writing a review on Amazon, Good Reads, Shelfari, Library Thing or other social media sites for readers will help the progress of independent publishing. To submit a review, go to the book page on any of the sites and follow the links for reviews. Books from independent presses rely on reader to reader communications.

Visit http://www.fomitepress.com/FOMITE/Our_Books.html for more information or to order any of our books.

As It Is On Earth
Peter M Wheelwright

Dons of Time
Greg Guma

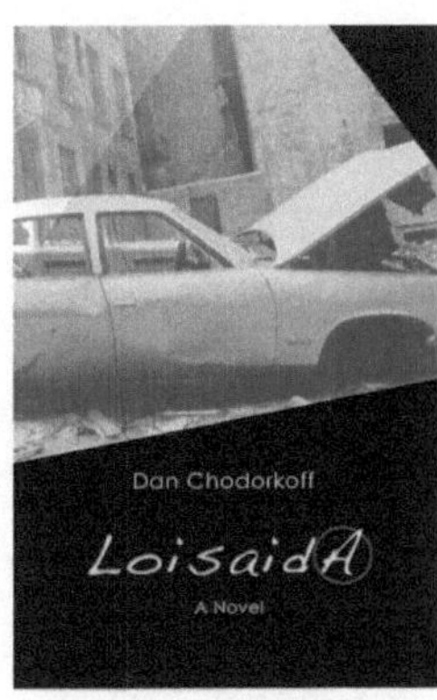

Loisaida
Dan Chodorkoff

My Father's Keeper
Andrew Potok

My God, What Have We Done
Susan V Weiss

Rafi's World
Fred Russell

Fomite

The Co-Conspirator's Tale
Ron Jacobs

Short Order Frame Up
Ron Jacobs

All the Sinners Saints
Ron Jacobs

Travers' Inferno
L. E. Smith

The Consequence of Gesture
L. E. Smith

Raven or Crow
Joshua Amses

Sinfonia Bulgarica
Zdravka Evtimova

The Good Muslim
of Jackson Heights
Jaysinh Birjépatil

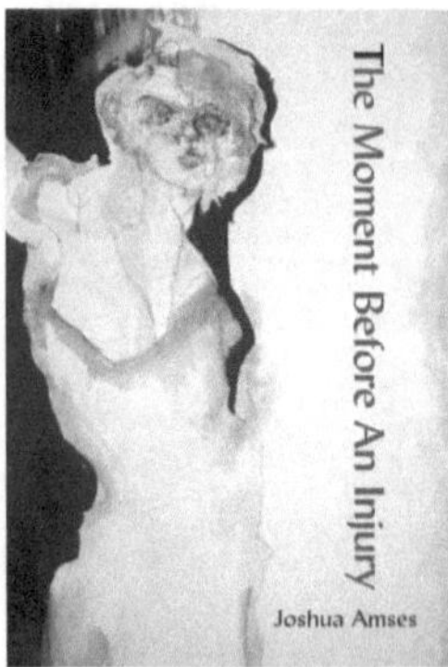

The Moment Before an Injury
Joshua Amses

The Return of
Jason Green
Suzi Wizowaty

Victor Rand
David Brizeri

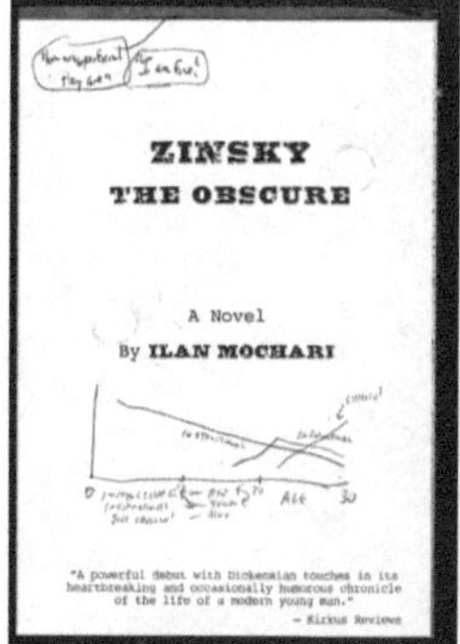

Zinsky the Obscure
Ilan Mochari

Body of Work
Andrei Guruianu

Carts and Other Stories
Zdravka Evtimova

Flight
Jay Boyer

Love's Labours
Jack Pulaski

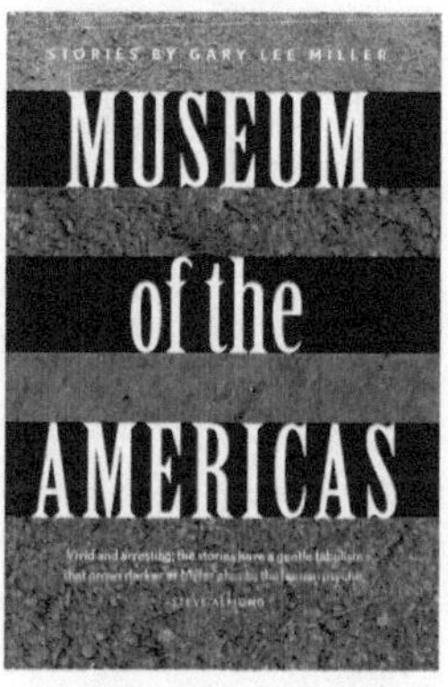

Museum of the Americas
Gary Lee Miller

Saturday Night at Magellan's
Charles Rafferty

Fomite

Signed Confessions
Tom Walker

Still Time
Michael Cocchiarale

Suite for Three Voices
Derek Furr

Unfinished Stories of Girls
Catherine Zobal Dent

Views Cost Extra
L. E. Smith

Visiting Hours
Jennifer Anne Moses

When You Remeber
Deir Yassin
R. L. Green

Alfabestiaro
Antonello Borra

Cycling in Plato's Cave
David Cavanagh

Fomite

AlphaBetaBestiario
Antonello Borra

Entanglements
Tony Magistrale

Everyone Lives Here
Sharon Webster

Four-Way Stop
Sherry Olson

Improvisational
Arguments
Anna Faktorovitch

Loosestrife
Greg Delanty

Meanwell
Janice Miller Potter

Roadworthy Creature
Roadworth Craft
Kate Magill

The Derivation of
Cowboys & Indians
Joseph D. Reich

Fomite

The Housing Market
Joseph D. Reich

The Empty Notebook
Interrogates Itself
Susan Thomas

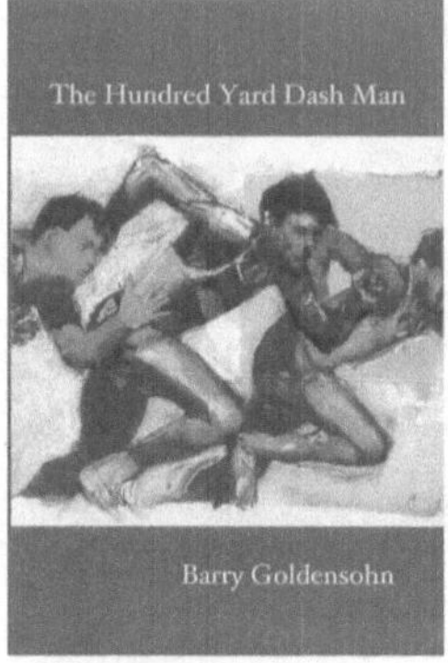

The Hundred Yard
Dash Man
Barry Goldensohn

The Listener Aspires
to the Condition of Music
Barry Goldensohn

The Way None
of This Happened
Mike Breiner

Screwed
Stephen Goldberg

Planet Kasper
Peter Schumann

My Murder
and Other Local News
David Schein

Picking Up the Bodies
James F. Connolly

The Falkland Quartet
Tony Whedon

Drawing on Life
Mason Drukman

Among Angelic Orders
Susan Thoma

Confessions of a Carnivore
Diane Lefer

Principles of Navigation
Lynn Sloan

Derail Thie Train Wreck
Daniel Forbes

Free Fall/Caída libre
Tina Escaja

A Guide
to the Western Slopes
Roger Lebovitz

Planet Kasper
Volume Two
Peter Schumann

Fomite

Nothing Beside Remains
Jaysinh Birjépatil

Foreign Tales of
Exemplum and Woe
J. C. Ellefson

Where There Are Two
or More
Elizabeth Genovise